# THE ADVENTURES OF
## Annie & Ellie-Belly

# THE ADVENTURES

*of*

# Annie &
# Ellie-Belly

## SHIRLEY SWINDLE

Boyle
& 
Dalton

Book Design & Production
Columbus Publishing Lab
www.ColumbusPublishingLab.com

Print ISBN: 978-1-63337-201-6
E-book ISBN: 978-1-63337-202-3

Printed in the United States of America

1 3 5 7 9 10 8 6 4 2

*In loving memory of my mother, the real-life Annie, who always had a twinkle in her eye and a prank up her sleeve.*

# CHAPTER 1
## Eggleton Farm

Six-year-old Annie grasped a limp string tightly and began to twirl her faded blue sunbonnet over her head like a cowboy preparing to release his lasso. Sweat trickled down the back of her neck like ants racing to a summer picnic.

"I'd just like to fling you plumb into the next county," she grumbled. "Ain't no sense in me havin' to wear a pesky ole bonnet ever' where I go."

But Mama had a notion that without a sunbonnet the hot summer sun would surely bake one's brain.

*It's a funny thing to me that Mama don't make Dan and Paul wear bonnets.* Annie tried to imagine her two older brothers out in the field, hoeing up and down the long rows of corn with cotton strings flapping around their chins from big puffy bonnets sitting high atop their heads. She laughed out loud at the picture dancing around in her mind.

"Where you been, Annie?" hollered Ellie from the front porch of the log cabin where the family lived. "And what's so funny?"

Ellie was only eleven months younger than Annie. In fact, it was not unusual for people to mistake them for twins. For one thing, they were about the same size, but more important-ly, they were always together. If you saw Annie, you could be sure that Ellie was not far behind. The two were not just sisters. They were playmates and best buddies.

"I been out yonder feedin' them ole chickens," replied An-nie. "Come on out here. I wanna show you somethin'."

Ellie scrambled down the steps and followed Annie. For Ellie, following Annie was as natural as breathing, although sometimes she ended up in a heap of trouble because of it. Not that Annie meant to get them into mischief. It was just that, somehow, mischief had a way of finding them, grabbing their hands, and dragging them along without them even realizing it.

"Hurry up, Ellie-Belly! You gotta see this," Annie urged.

Annie led the way back along the dusty trail toward the chicken house where a handful of hens pecked contently at the ground where she had recently scattered handfuls of corn. Out to the side of the henhouse sat Papa on an old tree stump, holding a squawking hen tightly under his left arm. With his right hand he flipped open his pocketknife and moved it toward the chicken's head.

"No, Papa! No!" screamed Ellie, running toward Papa as fast as her chubby legs would carry her. "Don't kill Rhoda just because she broke her beak and can't eat corn. I'll find a way to feed her. I promise I will. Don't hurt her, Papa!"

"Hold on, Little Bit. Quit your screamin'. I'm not gonna hurt Rhoda. I'm gonna help her. All I'm gonna do is trim her upper beak down to the size of the broken one so's she can pick up corn again. It won't hurt her one bit. It'll be just like you trimmin' your fingernails. Just give me a minute and she'll be scratchin' and peckin' right alongside them other hens out there."

True to his word, Papa quickly performed his surgery on Rhoda. He turned the little hen loose and stood to put his knife back in the pocket of his faded blue overalls. With a squawk

3

and a flap of her rusty brown wings, Rhoda scurried over to the other hens, searching for any stray pieces of corn they might have left behind.

"Here you go, Rhoda." Ellie squatted down, held out a handful of corn, and squealed with delight as the little brown hen ran over and began pecking hungrily at the golden kernels.

"She's eatin', Papa! She's eatin'!"

"Yep! Jus' like I told you she would, Little Bit," declared Papa as he headed out to the tobacco field.

Annie laughed at Rhoda's head bobbing up and down as the hen pecked away at the corn.

*Hmm, I wonder how Rhoda would look wearin' a bonnet?* she mused.

Annie never understood much about what caused the Great Depression of 1929. She hadn't the slightest notion of what the stock market was all about. And bank closings. Shucks! Who needed a bank? Banks were for people with money. Annie knew that much. But money was as scarce as hens' teeth around their house. She'd heard Papa talking to Mama about so many men, including himself, losing their jobs down at the cotton mill where they earned fifty cents a day. Annie knew that Papa worked long and hard for that fifty cents a day, and now, even that was gone. They wouldn't be able to pay the rent on the house in town anymore.

"Pack up, Mama, we're movin'," Papa had announced a few days ago.

Annie was used to moving. They'd moved all over the little town of Draper in Rockingham County, wherever Papa could find a place for them to live while he worked as a loom mechanic at the cotton mill. Annie never really minded moving from place to place. She had an imagination as big as all outdoors, and each new move provided opportunities for new adventures. With Papa's announcement, Mama drew a deep breath and let out a long sigh, while the corners of Annie's mouth turned up ever so slightly.

Within a week, the family had moved out to the country to a place called Eggleton Farm where Papa became a sharecropper. Mr. Eggleton owned the land and the log house they moved into. Papa would farm the land, and in the fall when the crops were harvested and sold, Papa would get half of the selling price. Annie knew her family was blessed to be able to live on the farm. What with having a vegetable garden, a cow, and a few chickens, they would at least have plenty to eat and milk to drink. People living in town were not so fortunate.

That night Annie tossed and turned on the big straw-tick mattress she shared with Ellie, thinking about their move to the country. She knew Mama hadn't wanted to move again, but sometimes blessings came in strange packages.

As Annie's eyelids began to droop she whispered into the darkness, "Jesus, thank you for your many blessings, even 'em ole bonnets…I think!"

## CHAPTER 2

# Corncob Wars

The next morning Annie sat quietly watching Papa wrap big white cloth bandages around his feet in place of shoes before going to the field to plow. He had something called athlete's foot that made his feet itch and swell so badly that sometimes he couldn't get his shoes on.

"Papa," Annie observed, "sharecroppin' ain't no easy way to make a livin', is it?"

"Well, no, Annie, it's not easy, but it'll put a roof over our heads and food on the table. Right now that's what matters to me!"

With that he stood up and hollered for Dan and Paul to meet him down at the barn to get started on the morning chores.

Annie and Ellie had their own share of chores to do, but for the two of them, life on the farm was one adventure after another. With Annie's creative imagination and Ellie's willingness to act as her accomplice, the two were never at a loss for ideas for fun and games. One of their favorite discoveries was an old abandoned car, sitting out in the side yard of the farmhouse, its rusty metal fenders torn off and lying haphazardly in the stubby grass nearby. As soon as she spied those fenders, Annie raced over to get a closer look.

"Well, looky here, Ellie-Belly!" called Annie. "This here's a rocky horse if ever I did see one. Come help me set this horse up on his feet."

Ellie scurried across the yard at Annie's bidding. Annie grabbed one end of the curved piece of metal while Ellie grabbed the other end.

"Over he goes!" yelled Annie.

With that, the girls flipped the fender over, then ran to flip the second one. Quickly each girl mounted her very own horse and began rocking away. Back and forth they rocked, singing at the top of their lungs, "Yankee Doodle went to town, ridin' on a pony. Stuck a feather in his hat and called it macaroni."

The girls were still riding and singing when their two brothers came walking into the yard carrying their hoes from the vegetable garden.

"Hey, Annie!" called Dan. "How's about a friendly little corncob fight?"

Dan and Paul seldom had time for games with the girls, so Annie and Ellie jumped at the chance for an afternoon of corncob fun. Neither Annie nor Ellie actually participated in the corncob fights, which took place on top of the nearby chicken house. It was their job to keep the boys supplied with ammunition to fight each other.

Corncobs lay strewn all over the dusty ground around the chicken house, so there was no lack of available bullets. The chicken house was made of old pine logs. Black tar paper covered the flat roof. Annie and Ellie loaded up their arms with the dry, scratchy corncobs and ran to the side of the chicken house. Annie stuck her bare feet between each log as she climbed swiftly up to the roof, being careful not to spill her armload of bullets. Ellie followed closely behind, her dress tail flying around her knees with each step. Up and down the side of the chicken house the girls climbed until they had stockpiled enough bullets for the war on the roof to begin.

Meanwhile, the two boys had climbed up to the roof and stood waiting, eager for Ellie to clap her hands as the signal to commence. Suddenly, corncobs were whizzing through the air like missiles.

"You better duck, Ellie-Belly!" Annie screamed with laughter.

Smack! Whop! Whack! One by one the corncobs found their mark or sailed over the roof of the chicken house to fall with a thump on the ground below.

"Hey, Paul, you missed me again!" teased Dan. "Ellie throws better than you!"

Paul grabbed two more cobs from the quickly diminishing arsenal. With a fast snap of the wrist, he let the next missile fly. This one caught Dan right between the shoulder blades as he turned to gather his own ammunition.

"Eee-oww!" yelped Dan, reaching around to rub his back.

Just then, Annie noticed that the stockpile of weaponry was getting smaller, so down the side of the chicken house she scooted and began quickly gathering up another armful of bullets.

Plop! A fat corncob fell to the ground beside her from the

war raging above. Annie was halfway back up the side of the chicken house, arms loaded to the brim, when she heard Papa's voice shouting from the yard below.

"Git down off that chicken house, Annie! What are you doin' climbing up there? You'll fall and break an arm. Now git down from there this minute!" The screen door banged a warning as Papa entered the house, tired from a long afternoon in the field.

A shocked Annie skinned backward down the logs until her feet touched the ground below. Mama knew the kids had corn-cob fights up there, but she'd never stopped them from their romp on the roof before.

*I guess Papa's never seen this game*, Annie thought as she watched the house closely.

She looked up at her siblings, now standing silently on the roof. For a few minutes nobody spoke a single word. Suddenly, Paul reached down and snatched another corncob, and immediately the war was raging again in full force. With a furtive glance over her shoulder, Annie drew a deep breath and started back up to the roof, holding tightly to her armload of cobs.

Just then, the screen door swung open and Papa's voice thundered through the afternoon air.

"Annie, I thought I just told you to stay off that roof! Young lady, you get yourself to this house on the double!"

Annie never did understand how she was the only one on the receiving end of Papa's fury that day. Papa usually scolded them with a finger thump on the head and a warning of, "You quit that, you little rascal, you!" Not this time, though. This time instead of a finger thump on the head, Annie got an honest-to-goodness, seat-burnin' spankin'.

*How come I'm the only one in trouble? I counted four soldiers in that war, but I seem to be the only prisoner!*

Meanwhile, the other soldiers had silently sneaked down the far side of the chicken house and gone their separate ways. Even Ellie had quietly returned to her newfound rocky horse friend, and was silently riding off into the sunset... without Annie.

Later that night, just before Annie's eyelids touched her cheeks in the darkness, she whispered, "Dear God, I've always heard big people say that all's fair in love and war. I guess that don't mean corncob war, huh, God?"

## CHAPTER 3

# Blackberries and Black-Draught

Annie could not remember ever going to the doctor for anything. When she or any other member of the family got sick, Mama always had some kind of home remedy on hand. One of the treatments Annie hated the most was what Mama called cleaning out week. About once a month everybody in the family had to take a dose of castor oil, Black-Draught, or a yucky white pill called a calley tab. Calley tabs were so bitter that you could hardly take a decent drink of water for a week afterward without tasting it still.

All three medicines made your tummy gripe and rumble something awful. But Mama thought they all had to be cleaned out on a regular basis. Mama called it purging. It was her way of making sure the family was clean from germs and toxins on the inside, and no amount of complaining could convince her otherwise. One thing was for sure; the path to the outhouse saw a lot of traffic during cleaning out week.

Early one morning before the sun had climbed very high in the sky, Mama handed Annie and Ellie each a half-gallon tin lard bucket and announced, "Come on, girls! We're goin' berry pickin'." She carried her own two-gallon water bucket across her arm as she led Annie and Ellie through grass drenched with early morning dew.

There was a huge blackberry patch down in the field below the house on Eggleton Farm. Annie looked forward to filling her bucket with that luscious purple-black fruit. She and Ellie ran ahead of Mama, eager to begin plucking the tender berries.

Plop! Plop! Went the berries as they hit the bottom of the empty pails. Except for Annie's pail. Annie plucked the tasty berries off the curling vines as fast as the prickly briars would allow. However, instead of filling her bucket, Annie was filling her mouth while purple juice trickled through her fingers and ran down her wrist. Annie didn't think she'd ever tasted berries quite so sweet. Ellie stuffed a handful of juicy berries into her mouth and then began filling her bucket. She loved blackberries as much as Annie, but she already felt the hot sun sending sweat trickling down the back of her neck. You could no longer hear the plopping sound the fruit made as it mounted higher and higher in her bucket.

Mama's hands moved swiftly from one long briar to the next, scooping berries into her bucket several at a time. After a while, she sat her bucket down, pulled a big handkerchief from her apron pocket, and wiped the sweat from her neck and face. It hadn't taken long for the morning sun to become a hot fireball, beaming down on the berry pickers.

"If we hurry, we can be through and back to the house before the sun gets much higher. These big berries make quick work of filling a bucket. How's your bucket look, Ellie?" Mama asked, looking across the patch at the girls.

Annie knew that Mama would soon be asking her the same question. She took a quick look into her bucket. Her stomach was beginning to feel a bit queasy. Staring into the bucket, Annie realized that not one single blackberry rested there. Every berry she'd picked had found its way into her mouth. All she had to show for the last half hour's work were stained fingers and purple lips.

Standing on her tippy toes, she quickly snatched at a cluster of berries hanging on a briar just above her head. No sooner had she plopped them into the bucket than Mama appeared at her side, peering into the nearly empty container.

"Land sakes, young'un! What have you been doin' the last half hour?"

Ellie stared in dismay at Annie's empty bucket and purple lips. Sissy was in big trouble and Ellie didn't know how to help her.

*Oh, goodness! I wish I'd emptied some of my berries into Annie's bucket.* But it was too late for that.

"Don't you know all them berries will make you sick, Annie?" Mama asked, shaking her head in disbelief.

"No, Mama. They tasted so good I just couldn't stop eatin' 'em," replied Annie.

"We'll take care of this when we get home, young lady," Mama promised.

A short while later, Annie trudged slowly back across the pasture carrying an empty bucket while Mama and Ellie balanced their full buckets of berries carefully by their sides.

True to her word, Mama took care of business when the trio reached the cabin. Down from the kitchen cabinet came the dreaded bottle of Black-Draught, and out came the big spoon.

*Surely Mama's not gonna give me Black-Draught*, Annie thought in dismay. *Surely 'em berries will clean me out good enough without any help from that medicine bottle.*

"Open up, Annie," ordered Mama.

Annie gagged as the smelly black powder touched her tongue. Away to the water bucket she flew, grabbed a dipperful of water and washed that nasty stuff down her throat.

"Mercy! That stuff's enough to kill a'body," Annie complained to Ellie. But she mustn't complain to Mama. She was in enough trouble without adding backtalk to her current situation.

Never could Annie remember her tummy rolling and griping the way it did that afternoon. While everyone else enjoyed steaming, hot blackberry cobbler for supper, Annie kept the path to the outhouse hot.

Later that night, she finally collapsed in an exhausted heap on the straw-tick mattress, hoping that Mother Nature had finished calling for one day. She'd not even felt like washing her dusty bare feet as she usually did before climbing into bed at night.

"My feet may be dirty," she mumbled to Ellie wearily, "but my insides are squeaky clean. That's for sure!"

# CHAPTER 4
## Sweet Secrets

The main crop grown on Eggleton Farm was flue-cured tobacco. Annie soon discovered that growing and harvesting tobacco was a community affair as well as a family affair. Neighbors would move from farm to farm helping each other. Everybody had a job to do, even two little barefoot girls.

When tobacco cutting time came, Papa and the boys used a little narrow sled called a submarine, which was pulled by a mule between the rows of tobacco. The men would pull the ripe yellow tobacco leaves off the stalk, pile them onto the sled, and leave the stalk standing in the field. When the sled was full they would haul the tobacco to the barn. There, Mama and the women would gather several tobacco leaves and hold them together at the top. Then they'd take another yellow leaf and wrap it around the top of the bundle and tie it all together. Annie thought it looked just like they were making tobacco ponytails. Then the leaves were strung in little bunches onto a tobacco stick and the men hung the sticks from rafters in the barn to dry.

Papa and Mama and the boys worked long hours in the barn alongside neighbors to get the tobacco ready for drying. The small barn was made of logs with a dirt floor. Inside, a brick tunnel called a flue ran eight to ten feet down each side of the barn. Each flue was connected to a huge firebox located outside the barn. A fire was built in each firebox to heat the flues and dry out the tobacco leaves hanging from the rafters above. Many loads of firewood were required to keep the fires burning. It usually took three to four days for the leaves to completely cure. The fire burned day and night until the tobacco was all cured. It was necessary for one man to stay in the barn at night to keep the fires burning, but often the men would buddy up and stay together, swapping tales and enjoying each other's company throughout the night.

During the day while the adults worked in the barn, Annie

and Ellie had their own job to do. Their job was to carry water from the spring to the barn for the workhands to drink. The barn was about a quarter of a mile above the house. The spring was down a long hill several hundred yards below the house in the opposite direction from the barn. So off they'd go, water buckets in hand, scuffling barefoot down the rocky path to the spring.

"Hey, Ellie, how did you and me get stuck with this job?" Annie complained one sultry afternoon.

"Don't know," Ellie answered, her little half-gallon bucket clanking against her bare leg with each step. "I heard Mama tell Mrs. Alice that we're too young to tie tobacco leaves, but we sure make dandy little water girls."

Annie thought it was a really hard job for two little girls, carrying heavy water buckets from the spring all the way up that steep hill to the barn every little bit. There had to be something they could do to make their job a mite more bearable.

Suddenly, Annie was grinning from ear to ear and a little chuckle escaped her lips. The chuckle was not lost on Ellie, who as usual was sticking to Annie like her shadow. Annie turned off the path and headed for the house.

"Come quick, Ellie. I got an idea."

"What are you thinkin', Sissy?"

"I'm thinkin' I shore would like a little somethin' for my sweet tooth right now. I'm thinkin' maybe we could stop by the house on the way to the spring and find us a little snack, so's we can have us a little more energy to tote this lard bucket full of water back up the hill to the barn, don't 'cha know?"

"But Sissy! You know good and well we ain't got nothin' sweet in the whole dadgum house, 'ceptin' them sweet taters Mama fried for breakfast this morning!"

"Nope! I don't want no sweet tater. I've had enough sweet taters. I'm about sick o' sweet taters!"

"Well, you know yourself, Sissy, Mama's been fixin' 'em sweet taters in place of bread, 'cause they ain't no flour to make biscuits," Ellie replied, kicking at a dirt clod with a bare foot.

Annie set her tin bucket down beside the path and motioned for Ellie to do the same.

"Yep, I got us a great idea, but you gotta promise you won't tell, Ellie."

Ellie glanced nervously over her shoulder even though they were well out of sight and earshot of the barn and the rest of the family.

"Sissy, you're not gonna get us in trouble again, are you? I ain't got no hankering to get on Mama's bad side and git a lickin' with that razor strop."

"Oh, shucks, little Ellie. Just do what I say and everything will be A-OK. The only lickin' we're gonna get is some white sugar lickin'. I've got us a plan, but we gotta hurry!"

With that, Annie grabbed Ellie by the hand and pulled her quickly up the front steps, across the porch and into the house. She headed straight for the kitchen with Ellie close behind. In a flash, Annie reached up into the cabinet and brought out two drinking glasses. Then she opened the pantry and took out the large glass jar where Mama stored her sugar.

"Run to the front porch and watch, Ellie. Make sure nobody's comin'!"

"Sissy, I'm afraid we're gonna get caught," squeaked Ellie.

"No, we ain't, Ellie. Now scat to the front door and stand guard!"

Obediently, Ellie took up guard duty at the front door. Annie ever so carefully lifted the sugar jar down off the shelf, opened the lid, and even more carefully began to fill the drinking glasses with that delectable white sweetness. Once the glasses were full, she wiped the lid and all around the edges of the sugar jar so as not to leave any telltale evidence of the theft. Back up to the top pantry shelf went the sugar jar. Now for two spoons. Annie's mouth began to water just looking at that glass of snowy whiteness.

Once they were back on the path to the spring, each girl pulled the handle of her tin water bucket over her arm so their hands could be free to dip their sugar snack, one delicious spoonful at a time, all the way to the spring.

When Annie stuck a sugar-coated tongue out at Ellie, Ellie laughed so hard her last spoonful of sugar came spewing back out of her mouth like a white cloud puff.

When the last granules had disappeared from their glasses, the girls filled their water buckets and hurried back up the path. When they reached the log cabin, they sat their water buckets down by the path, ran into the house, washed their drinking glasses and placed them back in the cabinet. Then they took that fresh spring water up to the barn, their sweet secret hidden deep in their tummies.

That was the first of several sugar thefts that occurred while Annie and Ellie were being dandy little water girls. Mama kept saying that something was a-goin' with her sugar, but she hadn't the slightest idea that the sugar thieves were living right under her very roof.

# CHAPTER 5

# Mr. Brown Shoes

Up in the barn the yellow tobacco leaves were beginning to turn brown as the heat from the fires slowly cured them. In a few days Papa and the boys would be taking the tobacco to market, hoping for a good profit for all their hard work. Since the flues were heated by externally fed fire boxes, the tobacco leaves would cure without being exposed to smoke. Flue curing produced a tobacco high in sugar with medium to high levels of nicotine. Most tobacco farmers preferred the flue-cured method because tobacco cured this way generally brought a better profit at market. That fact alone made working and sweating in the hot barn a little more bearable. Stopping by the water bucket for a dipperful of fresh, cold spring water also helped a'body tolerate the heat a bit better. So as long as the workers were still laboring in the barn, those dandy little water girls kept the spring path hot as well, bringing much-needed refreshment to the parched lips of the workhands.

It was on one of these many trips that the water brigade nearly met their own waterloo. Annie and Ellie had just made their routine stop by the kitchen, filled up their glasses with sugar, and walked back out the front door when an old black car chugged its way into the front yard and stopped amid clouds of dust.

Annie's heart froze in her chest. Very seldom did they ever see a car, especially way out here in the country. Without a word, Annie snatched Ellie's arm, dragged her around the side of the house, and pushed her silently into the chimney corner out of sight. They would just hide behind that big rock chimney until whoever was driving that car went away. Both girls listened breathlessly as someone pounded on the front door.

"Hey there! Anybody home?" they heard a strange man's voice call out.

Annie raised a silent finger to her lips as she stared down into Ellie's frantic face. Just then Annie heard the crunch, crunch of footsteps coming around the side of the house toward the chimney. There was just enough time for the girls to crawl under the floorboards of the back porch. Annie ducked down to scramble into the dark hideout when she heard Ellie whimper behind her.

"I can't, Sissy. I can't crawl in that hole. It's dark in there and there's big spiders in there!"

As Annie peered out at her sister in disbelief, she saw a large pair of brown shoes come to a halt right beside Ellie's small, bare feet. Annie's heart was thundering in her ears as she dragged herself out from under the floor. There stood Ellie, like a frightened little field mouse, staring up into the face of the stranger, feet glued to the spot, still holding her glass of sugar in her trembling hands.

Somehow Annie had managed to keep most of her own sugar in the glass during her mad dash under the floor. There they were. Caught red-handed, both holding evidence of their theft in shaking hands. Surprisingly enough to Annie, Mr. Brown Shoes didn't seem to notice their glasses of sugar, nor did he comment on Annie's unsuccessful attempt to hide.

"Where are your parents?" Mr. Brown Shoes asked, looking around the house.

"They're right up there at the barn," Annie managed to whisper. Her throat felt as dry as dust.

Mr. Brown Shoes turned and began walking quickly up the hill. Annie stared, wide-eyed as he disappeared out of sight up the path to the barn. She was sure that he would tell Papa and Mama about his encounter with two little girls eating sugar out of drinking glasses down at the house.

For some, the fear of what was to come once Mama found out about the sugar would have been enough to cause the stolen treat to lose its sugary appeal. But not for Annie.

"Shucks, little Ellie-Belly. If we're gonna get killed for this anyway, we might as well enjoy one last little glass before we die. Hey, I bet I can eat mine faster than you!"

The girls arrived at the barn moments later, just in time to hear Papa say, "Well, I don't know how that fella thought I was gonna buy his insurance. I don't hardly have enough money to buy flour, sugar and coffee, much less insurance."

Annie cast a sideways glance at Ellie as the two set their water buckets down on the wooden bench just inside the barn door.

"Well, I've done about all I can do up here today," Mama spoke up. "I'd best get on down to the house and fry up some more sweet taters. Supper'll be ready in about half an hour. Come on, girls, let's head that way."

The girls followed Mama back down the worn path, hardly daring to look at each other for fear that their secret would somehow escape. Slowly, Annie began to breathe a little easier.

Supper came and went without another word from Papa or Mama about their afternoon visitor. Annie and Ellie washed up the dishes and put them away with no complaining. Later, they hurried into their nightgowns and crawled into the big straw-tick bed that awaited them. Ellie began snoring softly almost as soon as her head hit the pillow. But for Annie, it seemed that a little prayer of thanksgiving was in order.

"Thank you, sweet Lord Jesus," whispered Annie into the dark, "for not lettin' Mr. Brown Shoes tell Papa and Mama our secret."

# CHAPTER 6
# Watermelon Caper

Papa rose early every morning and built a fire in the cookstove, then hurried out to the barn to milk the cow. When the fire was roaring in the stove, Mama would get up and cook breakfast. By the time Papa returned to the house with a pail full of warm milk, Mama would have a pan full of gravy ready, along with a bowl full of scrambled eggs. She'd pull a steaming pan of biscuits out of the oven when she had flour to bake them. Flour was not rationed down at the store as some items were, but Papa didn't always have money to buy it. As soon as breakfast was ready the girls tumbled quickly out of bed and headed to the kitchen. There was no lying in bed when Mama called for them to rise and shine. Once breakfast was over, Annie and Ellie cleared the table and began their morning chore of washing up the breakfast dishes. They knew the morning routine well. Get up. Eat breakfast. Wash dishes. Make the bed. Sweep the floor and go get water from the spring. And yet, every morning without fail, Mama would remind them as they stood up from the breakfast table, "Now girls, get to your dishes."

Washing dishes was Annie's least favorite chore. She'd been doing it since she was so little that Mama had put the dishpan of hot, soapy water down in a chair for her to reach. She would wash, Ellie would rinse and dry, and they'd both put the dishes away. Once the breakfast dishes were washed and put away it was time to make their bed. The straw tick they slept on was made of two big sheets sewn together with a big split down the middle where the straw was stuffed in. Every morning the girls had to try to stir up the knotty, bumpy straw and smooth the lumps out for the next night's sleep. Once that was over and the floors were swept, it was time to head down-hill to the spring to fetch water. There was no indoor plumbing in the house on Eggleton Farm.

Annie and Ellie scurried off to the spring this morning to

replenish the drinking water at the house. It was, however, the last day they would have to carry water up to the barn. The next day Papa and the boys would be taking the cured tobacco to market.

*Oh, happy day!* thought Annie as she set the water bucket down in the kitchen. Just then she heard a whistle coming from the front yard.

"It's Louise, comin' to play, Annie!" shouted Ellie with delight.

Louise was older than Annie and Ellie, but they loved to play with her. She was the only neighbor kid who lived close enough for them to play with. Her parents were helping Papa and Mama up in the tobacco barn that day. Annie and Ellie looked up to Louise, partly because she was older than they were, and partly because she was a daredevil. She'd do things that Annie and Ellie would never even think about, much less actually do. That day was no exception.

"Hey, where you off to?" Louise asked, ignoring the water buckets in their hands. "You girls wanna have some fun?"

"Sure, we wanna have fun, but we gotta carry water up to the barn," Annie replied.

"OK. I'll go with you, then I'll show you where the fun is."

Annie and Ellie quickened their pace to the spring, wondering what Louise had up her sleeve this time. Surely she wouldn't try to get them to dip snuff again like she had the last time they'd played with her.

Louise dipped snuff like an adult. A few days ago, she'd told Annie and Ellie how good it tasted and how they should try it. Mama kept her snuff up on the mantle over the fireplace, and since Mama was working up in the barn the girls had the perfect opportunity to try it upon Louise's suggestion. So Annie climbed up on a chair and brought the small brown glass down to the table. Louise showed them how to scoop a little bit out and tuck it into their lips. In a matter of seconds, both Annie and Ellie were gagging and spitting trying to get that awful-tasting stuff out of their mouths. Off to the kitchen for a dipperful of water they raced. Annie thought she was going to throw up, and Ellie yelled, "My mouth's on fire, my mouth's on fire!"

Louise just stood there doubled over with laughter while the girls tried desperately to wash that foul stuff out. No! Annie would not be trying that stuff again any time soon. As a matter of fact, not ever again!

After the buckets were filled with fresh, cold water, the girls started back up the path with Louise leading the way. Soon they were passing by a melon patch that stretched out to the right of the path.

"It sure is a hot day," Louise quipped. "A good watermelon would hit the spot about now. Set your water buckets down and let's go find us one. Last one to pull a melon's a rotten egg!" And off she ran, looking for a watermelon to pull off its vine.

The best watermelons had already been harvested, and every one the girls found and busted open was green, not fit to eat.

"Shucks, Louise, this ain't much fun if you ask me," remarked Annie. "None of these ole melons are worth eatin'."

With that Annie headed back to the path with Ellie close behind. Both girls had juice stains creeping down the front of their dresses from breaking open the faulty melons. No way to hide that from Papa and Mama. Annie wished with all her heart they had not let Louise talk them into stopping by that blasted melon patch. They were sure going to be in big trouble.

By the time they arrived at the barn, the water in their buckets was warm from sitting so long in the hot sun while the girls searched through the melon patch. Mama walked up with sweat running down her face, eager for a big dipperful of fresh, cold spring water. Suddenly, she spewed the whole mouthful back out onto the ground and turned around angrily.

"What in the world are you girls doin' bringin' hot water up here for us to drink?" she thundered.

Shortly afterward, two tearful little girls were on their way back to the spring for fresh water without Louise.

"Ellie-Belly, I think I'm gonna just sit down in that spring water when I get there!" Annie cried.

"Me too, Annie! My bottom's never been this hot!" Ellie sobbed.

Later that night, soft starlight spilled through the window onto the faces of two dandy little water girls who had learned an important lesson. Hot Mamas need cold, cold water to drink!

## CHAPTER 7
# Cool Our Rabbits

Work up in the tobacco barn had finally come to an end. Fires no longer burned in the fireboxes and the brick flue tunnels no longer warmed the inside of the small barn. The cured tobacco had been stacked on huge flat tobacco baskets, loaded onto wagons and hauled to the big tobacco warehouse in Durham. Papa's and the boys' attention had turned to harvesting the vegetables remaining in the garden closer to the cabin. Neighbors had returned to their own farms to gather in the last of the vegetable crops and prepare for winter just around the corner. Autumn had slowly begun to paint leaves red and yellow in the trees around the cabin. There was a nip in the morning air; enough to cause Annie and Ellie to pull on their high-topped leather shoes before going out to play.

The sun peeped over the horizon, promising to warm the day ahead on Eggleton Farm. The girls had finished their morning chores and wandered out to play along the well-worn spring path. Brown-winged grasshoppers fluttered into the air, startled by two sets of leather shoes scuffling along through brown stubby grass.

Annie reached up and jerked her faded blue sunbonnet off her head and turned it upside down. Then she began gathering small pebbles and tossing them into her bonnet. Ellie hastily followed suit. Soon the girls had their bonnets full of stones; plenty to separate the rooms in a pretend playhouse.

"See that big shade tree over there, Ellie?" asked Annie. "That's a splendid place to build a playhouse."

Soon the days would be too cold for building outdoor playhouses, but that day was perfect. Not a cloud in the sky and the sun toasty warm. A little bit too warm, Annie decided later that morning, to have on high-topped leather shoes.

Annie plopped down on the scratchy grass and began pulling at the leather strings. With a tug and a toss the shoes landed helter-skelter in the dry grass near the path. Annie giggled as the coarse grass tickled her sweaty toes.

"Go on, Ellie. Take your shoes off and give your toes some air," laughed Annie.

In the shake of a sheep's tail, two pairs of shoes lay abandoned by the spring path. Soon the playhouse was taking shape under the big oak tree. Rocks served as walls to divide the different rooms. Ellie found some nice green moss, which quickly became soft beds for their dolls. Cabinets for the kitchen and dining room were built using small scrap boards Papa had thrown onto the woodpile out back. Ellie found a pasteboard box on the back porch and it became their kitchen table. A careful search around the yard yielded several pieces of a broken dish. These were carefully placed on the kitchen table. A small tree limb served as a broom. With the beds made and the kitchen in order, it was time to go to the market for food. Annie turned her bonnet over, shook out the dirt from the pebbles they'd collected, and then plopped it back on her head.

"Here, Annie," called Ellie. "I found some eggs."

Ellie's hands grasped a big stem of fluffy yellow goldenrod

blooms. Meanwhile, Annie was pulling rough brown pieces of bark from a nearby maple tree.

"Here's the bacon to go with our eggs," replied Annie. "We'll need some healthy greens too. I'll gather some fresh kale for our supper."

And, of course, since no meal is complete without dessert, Annie and Ellie were soon making pies and cakes with sand, moistened with water from the nearby creek. Each cake was carefully decorated with brightly colored flower petals pulled from little patches of fall wildflowers, which grew along the path to the spring.

"Now where did you put that fruit jar, Ellie?"

Annie had found a quart fruit jar on the back porch. She knew just where Papa kept his hammer. With one good whack she drove a big nail through the jar lid to make a round hole. Next, she filled the jar with soapy water and tightened the lid. Off to the playhouse she scampered with her newly made churn. She laid it gently beside the trunk of the oak tree. It was time to churn the milk.

"You do the churning, Annie, and I'll be cookin' supper," Ellie offered.

Annie spotted a thin stick lying in the grass nearby. Just what she needed for a dasher to churn her milk. Into the hole in the lid went the dasher and the churning began. The liquid inside the fruit jar began to bubble and foam. Just then, the girls heard Mama calling from the cabin.

"Come to dinner, girls!"

Reluctantly the girls left their playhouse and trudged up the dusty path to the cabin. It would not do for them to ignore Mama's summons and be late for dinner. Besides, cooking up all that imaginary food down in the playhouse had made Annie and Ellie hungry for the real thing.

After dinner was over and the dishes were washed and put away, the girls hurried back outside to make the best of this warm autumn day. Annie was ready for an afternoon adventure.

"Ellie-Belly, I think I wanna go rabbit huntin'. How 'bout you?"

"Yea! Rabbit huntin'! Me too!" Ellie shouted.

"Here's me a stick and you a stick, Ellie. These are our guns. Now when you see a rabbit, shoot it quick before it hops away!" instructed Annie.

Off down the path the girls crept, hands cupped above

41

their eyes looking all around for a brown ball of fur to shoot. Suddenly, Annie spotted the high-topped brown leather shoes they'd thrown off their feet earlier that morning, lying beside the spring path, baking in the hot sun.

"Rabbits, Ellie! See those rabbits? Shoot, Ellie, shoot 'em! Shoot 'em dead!"

"Bang! Bang! Bang!" both girls shouted as they ran quickly over to the brown "rabbits" to make sure they were dead.

"We're dandy good shooters, Ellie-Belly. They're all four dead."

Annie reached out and touched one rabbit and jerked her hand back quickly.

"But they sure are hot rabbits! I think we're gonna have to cool 'em off before we can skin 'em. And I know just how to do it."

Throwing her stick gun down on the ground, Annie picked up two of the rabbits by their long brown laces. Ellie picked her rabbits up by their laces as well, and off to the creek they skipped, rabbits swinging by their sides. Once they arrived at the creek, Annie looked for a good place to wade in. Soon both girls were dipping their rabbits in the cool swirling water.

"Cool our rabbits! Cool our rabbits!" the girls repeated as they watched that cold water run over the hot brown pieces of leather. What fun it was, splishing and splashing in the creek while startled spring lizards darted from rock to rock, driven from their watery hideouts by wildly kicking feet.

As soon as all four rabbits were completely soaked, Annie decided they were cool enough to skin, so she and Ellie waded carefully back out of the icy water. Ellie followed Annie back up the path to the house, each girl carrying her rabbits over her shoulder. Annie thought it had been a very successful hunt. That is, until Mama saw their dripping rabbits hanging from their wet shoulders.

"What in the tarnation have you done to your shoes, girls?" Mama questioned in amazement.

"Annie said they looked like rabbits, Mama, and we shot 'em," offered Ellie. "And then we had to cool 'em off in the creek so's we could skin 'em."

"Well, if that don't beat all!" Mama spluttered. "The only pair of shoes you have, and now they're ruined. Lay them right here in the sun. We'll have to let them dry out, but I doubt if you'll be able to wear them when they do."

Unfortunately for the girls, Mama's prediction came true. When the "rabbits" were finally dry, the leather had drawn up so much that the shoes no longer fit either girl.

Annie's family hardly ever left the farm to go anywhere, and that was a good thing. Annie and Ellie had to go barefoot the rest of the fall. When cold weather arrived, and frost was nipping at their toes, Papa finally had saved enough money to buy the girls new shoes for winter.

"Might as well have skinned 'em ole rabbits for all the good they were when they dried," Annie decided. It was a good long while before she and Ellie went rabbit hunting again.

## CHAPTER 8

# Papa's Announcement

Winter was blowing its icy breath over the fields and through the treetops on Eggleton Farm. Papa had just returned from the country store where he'd gone to sell eggs and buy coffee and sugar.

"That's the last eggs I'm sellin' for twelve cents a dozen," he puffed. "We'll eat them ourselves before I'll sell them that cheap. I've never seen so many empty shelves down at the store. No coffee, no sugar and no lard! They've spread big towels over the empty counters. Mama, we'll just have to keep toastin' ground barley to mix with what little coffee we have left. I know it don't taste too good, but it'll have to do for now. I reckon we still got some molasses for sweetenin' since we've run out of sugar."

Annie stole a swift glance across the room at Ellie sitting as still as a mouse, watching the roaring fire crackle in the big stone fireplace. Mama had never solved the case of the missing sugar, much to Annie's relief, and both girls' lips were sealed. Annie slowly ran her tongue over her lips, remembering the sweet taste of those stolen sugar crystals. Ellie's eyelids were drooping as the warmth from the fire surrounded her like a cozy blanket. No need to worry about her exposing their little secret.

Things had not turned out so well for Papa sharecropping on Eggleton's farm. He, Mama and the boys had worked so hard raising the tobacco crop and preparing it for market. Yet, when the crop was sold the prices were down, and the money he'd made hadn't even been enough to cover the cost of the fertilizer he had used in growing the tobacco. Papa's next words caught Annie's full attention.

"Mama, you'd better start packin' up tomorrow. I hear work has picked up at the cotton mill and we're movin' back to town. I'll go back to work at the mill and the kids can get started to school."

School! Here it was, already December, and Papa wanted them to start to school! The very idea seemed crazy to Annie. Whoever heard of starting to school in December? Annie had turned eight years old back in July and had never been to school a day in her life. *Startin' to school at eight years old and I'm already missin' the first three months. Oh dear!* Annie thought to herself. One minute Annie wanted to jump up and down and shout, "Yippee!" and the next minute she was ready to crawl up under her old lumpy straw-tick bed and never come out.

A while later Annie snuggled up close to Ellie, trying to warm herself between the cold straw tick and the sheet.

"Wonder what it'll be like, Ellie, goin' to school for the first time? I'm a little bit scared. Are you? But at least we'll be together."

Ellie's only response was a soft little snuffle-like snore. Finally, Annie's own snuffle joined Ellie's and another day had ended on Eggleton Farm.

## CHAPTER 9
# Back to Town

A gray December dawn awakened Annie the next morning even before Mama's call to "rise and shine." She reached over and shook Ellie awake.

"Get up, Ellie. We're movin' back to town today and you and me got us some last minute explorin' to do before we go. Hurry up!"

Annie knew she and Ellie would have to complete their morning chores first, then maybe Mama would let them grab their coats and head outside for one last adventure on the farm before climbing up into the wagon for the bumpy trip to town. Papa and the boys were already loading the family's belongings in the rickety old farm wagon Papa had borrowed from

Mr. Eggleton. Mama was hurrying to fix a pan of sawmill gravy. There wasn't enough flour for biscuits, but the chickens had supplied them with enough eggs to feed the family. It only took a spoonful or two of flour to make the gravy, and hot gravy poured over eggs would make a hearty meal for the family this morning.

Annie and Ellie dressed quickly. No need to fool with trying to smooth out the straw tick this morning. Mama would be adding fresh straw to the tick once they arrived at the house in town. The girls hastily swallowed their helping of eggs and gravy, eager for the rest of the family to finish eating. Soon they were washing their last panful of dishes in the log cabin on the farm. Annie grabbed the broom and gave the floors one last good sweeping before standing the tattered broom up in the corner of the kitchen.

"Mama, can me and Ellie go play 'til we have to leave?" Annie pleaded.

"I reckon you can," Mama replied. "But mind that you don't get in Papa's way gettin' that wagon loaded, you hear?"

"We won't, Mama," Ellie promised.

Once outside, Ellie suddenly spotted Rhoda out in the

chicken pen scratching at the cold, hard ground for a bug or grain of corn.

"Oh, Rhoda," she wailed. "I'm gonna miss you, you ole raggedy bunch of feathers, you!" She ran over and scooped Rhoda up in her arms, much to the little hen's surprise. With a lurching and flapping of wings, Rhoda managed to free herself from Ellie's clutch and flew squawking toward the safety of the henhouse.

"Sure hope Mr. Eggleton takes good care of you," Ellie mused sadly.

Meanwhile, Annie was on her way to the creek below the springhouse. When Ellie caught up to her, she was turning rocks over with a splish here and a splash there.

"Jus' wanted to catch me one more lizard before we have to leave the creek," Annie puffed. "But I think they must be hibernatin' or something. I ain't found one yet."

"Hey, Annie. Let's go ride our rocky horses one last time before Mama hollers for us to go," Ellie begged.

"Oh, all right, Ellie-Belly. Ain't got no more time to spend here chasing 'em ole lizards anyway."

Back up the spring path the girls ran, hoping for one more

good ride before Papa called them to board the wagon. Around the side of the house they ran to where their horses stood ready. The rusty metal made for a cold ride, but the girls didn't care. They rocked back and forth, urging their horses on as they sang their favorite "Yankee Doodle" song at the top of their lungs.

All too soon it was time to say goodbye to Eggleton Farm. Annie's eyes filled with unbidden tears as she climbed aboard the wagon, filled to the brim with their meager household belongings. Even though Papa, Mama, and the boys had had to work very hard on the farm over the last year, Annie and Ellie had enjoyed one exciting adventure after another; hunting rabbits along the spring path, playing house under the big shade tree, and riding their fender rocky horses. And last but not least, licking sugar out of tall kitchen glasses and never getting caught! Annie slowly lifted her hand and waved a sad farewell as the team of horses clip-clopped the family down the bumpy road, leaving Eggleton Farm and all those adventures behind.

## CHAPTER 10
# The Mill Village

Ellie and Annie crawled into a little hole underneath a couple of chairs in the back of the wagon and settled down for the ride into town. Meanwhile, Mama found a spot between some boxes piled high with pots and pans. The boys sat with Papa up on the bench seat behind the horses. Ellie snuggled up close to Annie, her coat pulled up to her chin as the wagon bumped and rattled along. They were heading toward a little four-room house on 400 Street.

The town was actually a mill village, which meant that all the houses around the cotton mill were owned by the men who owned the mill. They rented the houses out to mill employees. The streets were identified by numbers instead of names.

Annie stared at the row of white frame houses as Papa turned the creaking wagon onto 400 Street. Almost all the houses were white, but here and there one was painted yellow. Annie crossed her fingers as the wagon rolled slowly down the street, hoping the house Papa stopped in front of would be yellow. Yellow reminded her of sunshine and fresh air and the countryside she'd just left.

"Whoa there!" Papa called to the horses. With a bump and a jolt the wagon came to a standstill in front of a white house, much to Annie's dismay. The houses were built side by side along the street with only a driveway separating them. Each house had a small front yard facing the street and a slightly larger backyard. Annie noticed that all the houses had a little path and an outhouse in the backyard as well. None of the houses were equipped with indoor plumbing. Annie watched curiously as a handful of people gathered around a long-handled water pump a few hundred feet down the street. Each person stood waiting his or her turn to fill a bucket with water from the pump.

"That's where our water comes from," Papa explained as he and the boys began unloading the wagon. "You girls won't have quite so far to carry it now."

Annie hadn't minded the trips to the spring to fetch water. There had always been some small critter like a grasshopper or a spring lizard to capture her attention along the way. But here, Annie could already tell there wasn't much to explore.

She shivered as Mama handed her and Ellie a box of clothes to carry into the house. Soon Mama was stuffing fresh straw into straw ticks and making up their beds. Papa and the boys brought the last pieces of furniture into the house and hurried back out to the street. They'd have to hurry to get the wagon back out to Eggleton Farm and return on foot before nightfall. Before he left, Papa started a fire in the fireplace to warm the house while Mama and the girls unpacked the boxes and put their belongings in order. It didn't take very long to slide what few clothes they had into drawers or cardboard boxes under the bed.

By the time Papa and the boys returned, most of the furniture was in place and Mama had supper ready on the woodstove in the kitchen.

"Mama, that pipin' hot cornbread and big bowl of buttered potatoes shore does smell mighty delicious. I'm as hungry as an ole she-bear!" declared Papa.

When supper was over, a tired Annie and Ellie were directed once more to their dishwashing chore.

"Some things jus' never gonna change," Annie whispered to Ellie, plunging her hands into the hot, soapy water.

## CHAPTER 11

# Surprised at School

Annie rolled over and tugged at Ellie's shoulder.

"Wake up, Ellie. Wake up! We're goin' to school today!"

Ellie bolted upright, rubbing the sleep from her eyes, then quickly tumbled out of bed after Annie. Mama had breakfast on the table when the girls bounced into the kitchen, eager to be off on a totally new adventure. Eight-year-old Annie was enrolling in school for the very first time, as was Ellie. Although it was already December, Papa and Mama saw no problem with enrolling the girls in school in the middle of the year. After all, it was more convenient now that they were living back in town and the girls could walk to school. It was Mama's intention to enroll both girls in first grade even though Annie was eleven months older than Ellie. Annie had no idea that this was not the way schools operated. Dan and Paul would be returning to classes in the same building, so Mama decided that the boys could take care of enrolling their sisters in school that morning. The girls skipped and laughed along the dusty gravel road. Papa had managed to buy each girl a little five-cent writing tablet and a penny pencil, which they clutched tightly in their hands as they skipped along.

As the girls approached the huge brick school building following closely behind Dan and Paul, their steps slowed ever so slightly as they gazed in awe.

"Come on, girls! Quit gawkin' and start walkin' or we're gonna be late," scolded Dan. "I have to get you two enrolled before I can go to my own class."

Annie grabbed Ellie's hand and together they followed Dan through the huge wooden doors and down a musty smelling hallway to the principal's office while Paul hurried off to look up some of his friends before the morning bell rang. Dan swung the office door open and there sat Mr. Daniels, the principal, busily shuffling through a stack of papers on his desk. As the three entered the room he peered over his wire-rimmed glasses and spoke pleasantly.

"Good morning. Please be seated and I'll be with you in just a moment."

Dan led the girls to a wooden bench pushed up against a wall in the small office. Annie and Ellie sat quietly, swinging legs that didn't quite touch the floor, hearts beating wildly as they waited for Mr. Daniels to speak again. Dan ran his fingers through his wavy blond hair, anxious to do his brotherly duty and be on his way to class. He could hardly wait to meet up with his own buddies whom he'd not seen since moving to Eggleton Farm. He glanced up as Mr. Daniels cleared his throat.

"Now what can I do for you folks today?" Mr. Daniels questioned as his eyes took in the three.

"Well sir," Dan began. "These here are my two sisters, Annie and Ellie. My name's Dan. I've been to this here school before. But this is their first time. Mama's feelin' poorly today so she told me to get them enrolled and started in first grade."

"I see," replied Mr. Daniels. "How old are you, Annie?"

Still clutching her pencil and writing tablet close to her chest, Annie looked up at Mr. Daniels and exclaimed, "I'm eight years old and Ellie here is seven." Annie squeezed Ellie's hand tightly and the corners of Ellie's mouth turned up shyly as she too stared up at Mr. Daniels. In just a few minutes she and Annie would be off to class together.

Wrinkle lines puckered Mr. Daniels' face as he looked from one smiling girl to the other.

"I'm sorry, girls, but we are overcrowded at our school this year. Now, by state law, I'll have to enroll you, Annie. But Ellie, you'll have to wait until next year to enroll in first grade. Now let's get some paperwork completed for you, Annie."

Annie and Ellie stood in front of Mr. Daniels' huge wooden desk, staring at him in disbelief. Surely they had not heard him correctly. Ellie raised her writing tablet up over her face and began to cry softly. The very thought of being left at home while Annie, her buddy, her best friend, went off to school brought a rush of salty tears streaming down her chubby little cheeks. Annie felt a sudden surge of anger as she stared at the man seated behind his desk.

"Mr. Daniels, sir," Annie blurted out, her words tumbling over each other in her frustration. "You don't understand. Ellie and I have to be together. We've never, ever been separated in our whole lives and I have to take care of her. I promise we won't be any trouble. Please, please let her stay!" Annie pleaded, lips trembling at the sight of Ellie crying behind her writing tablet.

"I'm sorry, Annie," Mr. Daniels replied. "I understand your wish to be together. However, rules are rules and I must abide by them. Dan, you'll have to walk Ellie back home. Tell your parents she'll have to wait until next year to start school."

Annie's feet felt like lead bricks dragging slowly down the hallway behind Mr. Daniels a few minutes later as he walked her to her new classroom. All she wanted to do was ball up her fists and pummel her new principal in the face. So much for the exciting new adventure she and Ellie had planned. A big lump rose in her throat when she pictured Ellie's tear-streaked face as Dan led her down the hallway toward the front door and home.

The rest of the day was a scary blur as Annie tried to make sense of what was happening around her. The anger she felt toward Mr. Daniels left a queasy feeling in her stomach which remained with her all morning long. Even though she was hungry at lunchtime, Annie did not feel like eating a bite of her steamy tomato soup. The saltine crackers and shiny apple remained untouched on her tray. Finally, she managed to swallow a few sips of milk to quiet the rumbling of her stomach.

It didn't take Annie long that first day to realize that she was the oldest one in the class of first graders and already half a year behind. The only book Annie had at her house was the Bible. No children's books with numbers, colors, shapes or letters were to be found there, and Mama had never thought it necessary for Annie and Ellie to learn those things before they started to school. How Annie wished she had just one book at home to call her own. With hardly enough money for food and shelter, books were just not something Papa and Mama felt necessary.

When the dismissal bell rang that afternoon, Annie dashed outside to wait for Dan and Paul, eager to get home to see about Ellie. Through the dusty streets she ran ahead of her brothers until she rounded the corner of 400 Street. As soon as she was in sight of the house she saw Ellie jump off the front steps and come running, arms outstretched, eager to hear Annie's account of the day. Arm in arm they skipped up the steps and into the little white frame house. They'd have to go their separate ways again, come morning. But for now they had each other and, after chores, there was playing to be done.

Sleep didn't come easily for Annie that night. Over and over in her mind she saw Ellie's face hiding behind her writing tablet as Mr. Daniels refused to enroll her in school.

"Dear God, you know how I always been takin' care of Ellie, all her life. Now I gotta go to school without her. Reckon you could spare an extra angel jus' to watch over her while I'm gone during the day? You know how busy Mama is, and... well, if you could jus' spare one little ole angel I'd be mighty grateful to you, sir."

For the first time all day, Annie felt a calm peace wash over her, and minutes later soft eyelashes were brushing her cheeks as sweet slumber carried her away.

# CHAPTER 12
# A Note, a Nurse, and a Needle

Annie's first two weeks of school were lonely without Ellie. Every morning she lagged several steps behind Dan and Paul as they made their way to school. School had lost its earlier appeal, and each day dragged on endlessly until the afternoon bell sounded and Annie could hurry home.

However, slowly but surely Annie began to make friends and adjust to a very crowded first grade classroom. Her teacher, Ms. Neil, worked patiently to help Annie learn the alphabet and write her numbers. Annie struggled to catch up with the other students who had the advantage of being there months before she arrived.

"Make the number eight like this," explained Ms. Neil as

her pencil moved smoothly in a figure eight. Annie quickly drew two circles, one atop the other, and looked up for Ms. Neil's approval.

"We'll keep practicing, Annie. I'm sure you'll get the hang of it soon."

Annie saw no good reason why two circles stacked one on top of the other would not work just fine for the number eight.

Her thoughts were interrupted by a light tapping on the classroom door. All heads turned to see a tall smiling lady dressed in white waiting quietly by the door.

Ms. Neil quickly called for those students who had brought a note from home that morning to line up. Annie looked down at her feet as several children walked up and formed a line at the front of the room. She knew she should be lining up with them, but somehow her feet felt glued to the floor and she couldn't move. She had brought a note from home for sure. That note gave the county health nurse permission to administer an immunization to Annie at school that day. Annie's heart thumped wildly in her chest as visions of long, sharp needles loomed menacingly in her head.

*Those big ole needles hurt bad, and besides all that, they make a big red lump on your arm, and then your arm gets so sore you can hardly move it for days. Nope, I ain't gettin' in that line,* Annie decided.

"OK, come along with me," directed the smiling nurse.

Reluctantly the line of fearful children followed her out the door and down the hall. Annie nibbled nervously on her finger-nails, wondering how in the world she was going to explain to Papa and Mama why she didn't get the shot like they'd intended her to do. She would get a lickin' for sure when they found out she had disobeyed. Even so, the thought of getting stuck in the arm with a sharp needle sent shivers of fear racing up and down her spine, and she decided a lickin' would be the better of the two evils she faced.

Annie's fingers trembled as she tried her best to focus on the assignment at hand. Suddenly Ms. Neil was standing beside her desk. Annie dared not look up, but kept writing feverishly until she heard her teacher's voice asking, "Annie, didn't you bring a permission note from home this morning? I thought I saw it earlier."

Annie thought she was going to faint. In fact, if she could only just faint right this moment, maybe she wouldn't have to answer Ms. Neil's question. How could she lie to Ms. Neil? She raised fearful eyes to her teacher and managed to squeak out a timid, "Yes, ma'am."

Gently, Ms. Neil took Annie by the hand and led her down the hallway in the direction the other children had gone.

They stood together in that line, Ms. Neil and Annie, with Ms. Neil firmly but gently holding Annie's hand. All too soon for Annie it was her turn to face the needle.

"Just relax, dear," smiled the nurse as she prepared to do her job. "It will all be over in just a few seconds."

*It sure will,* Annie thought, *'cause I'm gonna have a heart attack and die right here in school when I see that needle.*

Just then Ms. Neil reached over and gently turned Annie's face toward herself. With a big smile she whispered, "I've got you, Annie. It's OK."

Annie felt the cool alcohol being rubbed on her arm, followed by a quick little bee sting feeling. Annie's breath caught in her throat for an instant. But then Ms. Neil was hugging her and patting her on the back, exclaiming something about her being such a brave little girl.

Annie didn't feel very brave walking back to class with the

other children. But she sure was happy about one thing. The note, the nurse, and the needle were behind her, and she didn't have to worry about getting that lickin' from Mama when she got home that day.

Later that night with Ellie snuggled up beside her in their straw-tick bed, Annie reached up and rubbed her finger across the small, round Band-Aid that covered the tiny needle prick. Her thoughts returned to her teacher's gentle hand turning her head away from the forthcoming needle. *Why, come to think of it, I didn't see that needle at all.*

"Thank you, Jesus," Annie whispered into her pillow, "for giving me Ms. Neil as my teacher. Dear God, she must be the bestest teacher in the whole wide world."

## CHAPTER 13

# Freckles and Buttermilk

A soft ray of starlight peeked through the window and spilled over onto Annie's cheek as she lay listening to the nightly ritual of the cricket symphony tuning up outside her bedroom window. Seemed like those spry little critters with their skinny legs, wiry antennae, and enormous bug eyes always waited until she crawled into the big old lumpy straw-tick bed to strike up their spring concerto. And if that wasn't enough to keep a person awake, there was Papa, engulfed in his huge, fluffy featherbed across the hall, snoring like a buzz saw with Mama's soft snuffle echoing closely behind.

*Tarnation! How's a girl supposed to get a wink of sleep?*

"Hey, Mr. God. Are you awake up there? 'Cause I'm wide awake down here! Seems like the whole world's asleep, but me."

With that Annie hugged her pillow tightly to her ears to muffle the crescendo of sound around her. Ordinarily the nightly song and dance of the crickets wouldn't have bothered her. In fact, sometimes it even lulled her to sleep. But that night was different. She could feel her cheeks turning red as she remembered the snickers of two of her classmates walking behind her in the crowded hallway after that day's dismissal bell.

"Can you believe she fell for that?" laughed the tall redhead, elbowing her companion.

"Nope, Sarah, I can't. But she's such a country bumpkin," replied Julie, knowing full well that this country bumpkin was walking just ahead of her down the crowded hallway hearing every word of their conversation.

"Just imagine smearing buttermilk all over your face to get rid of freckles." With that, both girls burst into fresh peals of laughter.

*How in tarnation did those two find out about the little buttermilk experiment in the first place? My brothers! It must've been one of my stupid brothers. Nobody else knew exceptin' Ellie-Belly. And Ellie always keeps my secrets.*

Lying there in the darkness Annie remembered the incident like it was yesterday. It had happened when they lived out on Eggleton Farm. Their neighborhood playmate, Louise, knew just how much Annie hated those blasted freckles that peppered her nose and cheeks like cinnamon on buttered toast.

"Hey, Annie," offered Louise one hot summer day. "I can tell you jus' exactly how to git rid of 'em silly freckles on your face. All's you have to do is rub buttermilk all over your face, let it dry good for one hour, and then wash it all off. It'll fade them freckles like they ain't never been there before." With a confident snap of her fingers she predicted, "Yessir, them freckles will fade away like snowflakes in July. You can take my word for it."

That was the best news Annie had ever heard. She figured Louise must know, because she didn't have nary a freckle on her suntanned face. And besides all that, Mama churned buttermilk almost every day.

The next afternoon Annie found the perfect opportunity to try Louise's surefire remedy for removing freckles.

"Come on, Ellie-Belly. You and me's got a job to do right now."

"Annie, are you gonna get us in trouble with Mama again?" questioned her younger sister.

"No, Ellie-Belly. Just do as I say."

Just then Mama came around the side of the house with an apron full of fresh-picked vegetables from the garden.

"Annie, you and Ellie take the water buckets to the spring and bring back some fresh water. I'm headin' in to cook supper. Now don't dally! Get to it!"

Annie hurried into the house to grab the water buckets, elated that Mama had just given her the perfect chore. The springhouse was where the buttermilk was kept. The big glass jars of buttermilk were stored in the springhouse until they were needed in the kitchen at mealtimes. Annie waited until Mama went to the woodpile to gather kindling to start the fire in the big black cookstove. Then she quickly grabbed a small tin cup from the cupboard and hid it inside her larger tin water pail.

Ellie grabbed the handle of her own water pail and scurried along beside Annie down the springhouse path. Annie glanced over her shoulder to make sure no one was following them. The girls could hear the rushing sounds of the creek as it made its way around the bend and down through the moss-covered springhouse, splashing over and around the big glass jars of milk where Mama had placed them on the wooden shelf Papa had built. Even in the summer the icy cold creek water moving constantly through the springhouse kept the milk and butter refreshingly cold. Good thing, too! Not many people Annie knew even owned a refrigerator. Refrigerators cost money and burned electricity, neither of which Papa and Mama had.

Annie set her bucket down, then reached down and pulled off the heavy, wet board that helped keep the milk jars in place under the swiftly moving water. She knew which jar Mama kept the buttermilk in. She ever so carefully lifted it out of the swirling wetness and placed it gently on the ground beside her. Then she reached into her empty water bucket and drew out the small tin cup she'd placed there earlier.

"Annie! What on God's green earth are you doin'?" Ellie's big blue eyes were fastened curiously on her older sister. "Mama sent us to get water, not buttermilk!"

"I know, Ellie. 'Member how Louise told me I could get rid of my freckles? Well, this here's how it's done. Now you just watch and make sure nobody's a'comin'."

At this, Ellie dutifully glanced over her shoulder, then assured Annie that they were in the clear. Using her cotton dress tail, Annie carefully wiped the water off the slippery jar, then deftly untied the string that secured the clean cloth Mama had placed over the mouth of the jar in place of a lid. Annie knew that things like canning lids were not to be found while the war was raging overseas. Anything metal was directed toward making weapons for the war effort, and many common household items had to be sacrificed to that cause. But right at that minute, Annie had a cause of her own.

After freeing the cloth from the mouth of the jar, she picked up the heavy load.

"Hold my tin cup up, Ellie, so's I can fill it with buttermilk. Hurry up!"

"How in the world you gonna get rid of freckles a'drinkin' buttermilk, Annie? And why don't you just wait and drink it at supper?"

"'Cause you don't drink it, Ellie-Belly. Now you jus' keep

a look-out so's nobody catches me. Mama'd flog me good if she saw me puttin' this stuff on my face."

Ellie watched, puzzled as Annie poured the milk out of the small tin cup into her hand, then reached up and rubbed the milky whiteness all over her face. Annie looked like a white-faced raccoon with tiny yellow specks of butter dotting her cheeks here and there. Ellie giggled, then burst out laughing at the spectacle before her.

"Hush," Annie sputtered. "Someone will hear you." Annie batted her eyelids furiously as she hurried to retie the cloth over the milk jar and set it back in its resting place in the springhouse. Tiny white droplets fell from her face into the gurgling water below. Her task accomplished, Annie stood up and reached for Ellie's hand.

"Now, we'll play in the creek while this stuff dries. Then, when I wash it off, my freckles will be all gone. Louise told me that's what she did, and I know it works. She has no freckles at all, Ellie!"

Slowly the milk began to dry on Annie's face as she and Ellie splashed in the creek, turning over rocks and laughing gleefully as spring lizards darted out, disturbed from their dark hiding places. Annie reached up and scratched her itching nose. She could hardly believe she'd done this. But it seemed such a simple thing. After all, she'd heard about a story in the Bible where God had told a man named Naaman to go dip himself in the muddy Jordan River to get rid of a disease called leprosy. Naaman finally obeyed and the leprosy had disappeared forever. Surely she could endure dried buttermilk for a few more minutes, hoping for her own miracle.

The sun soon dried the buttermilk on Annie's face until it cracked like clay in a long summer drought. When she could stand the itchy tightness no longer, Annie scooped up handfuls of cold creek water and splashed them across her face seven times, just as Naaman had dipped himself in the Jordan River seven times and come up clean. At last, her face was squeaky clean without a trace of the sticky whiteness left.

"What? What's wrong with my face, Ellie?"

"Nothin', nothin's wrong with your face, Annie. It's just like before. Your freckles are still there. They jus' look cleaner now, that's all."

With a sick feeling in her tummy, Annie knew she'd been had.

*Blast that Louise! She's always gittin' us into trouble of some kind.*

So why did Annie think this time would be any different? Louise had known all along that crazy trick wouldn't work. And Annie had fallen for it! Not only that, but she and Ellie had caught a scolding from Mama when they'd finally gotten back to the house with the water she'd been waiting on.

"You big lame brain, Louise!" yelled Annie the next day as Louise ventured warily over across the front yard. "You knew buttermilk wouldn't take these stupid freckles away."

"Aww, I was jus' funnin' you, Annie. Don't be gittin' yer tail feathers all ruffled. Sides all that, Dan and Paul thought it was pretty funny too!"

Lying there beside Ellie in the darkness, it seemed Annie could still hear Louise's cackling laughter. And yes, she was sure her big dumb brothers had told Sarah and Julie all about it and they were all getting a good laugh at her expense.

*It's OK,* she thought smugly as she hugged her pillow a little tighter over her ears. *What goes around comes around.*

"Mr. God, is that in the Bible?"

## CHAPTER 14
# School Bus Stowaways

The sun was hanging around a little longer each day, and the school year had drawn to a close. Annie thought it was a pretty short year, seeing as how she'd only been enrolled since December. But oh how happy she was to be able to romp through those lazy, happy days of summer with Ellie.

The girls had new places to explore since Papa, once again, had moved the family back out to the country. Each new morning brought a rush to get chores done. The sooner the chores were done, the sooner Annie and Ellie could be off on another round of exploring. There were new playhouses to build and June bugs to catch. Annie taught Ellie how to catch those big green June bugs and gently tie a string around one back leg, then turn the bug loose to fly away, only to be caught when it reached the end of the string. Who needed a paper kite when you could have a real live kite zooming over your head, round and round up in the sky? Ellie loved the flying part, but sometimes that darned bug would zoom down and light on your head, or your arm, or somewhere else on your body, dragging its scratchy little insect legs over your skin. That part gave Ellie the shivers and she'd scream, "Annie, get this thing off a'me, right now!"

Ellie much preferred catching fireflies at dusk. They were small and sleek and their legs were not at all stiff and scratchy like June bugs' legs. After they'd caught a dozen or so and put them into the glass Mason jar Mama gave them, they'd sit down on the front porch and watch the soft blink blink from their firefly lamp as it cast a tiny glow in the evening shadows.

Summer passed all too quickly for Annie, and soon the hot, humid days gave way to milder temperatures and cooler nights. Trees dressed themselves once again in scarlet, brown and gold, while the autumn sky took on that deep azure blue only seen in the fall of the year.

This year when school opened, Annie and all her siblings began the school year together. Even though Annie and Ellie were not in the same grade, each one knew that the other was somewhere in the same building, and when the afternoon dismissal bell rang, they'd be walking home together.

A school bus ran by their house, but the children chose to walk to and from school every day. Annie's and Ellie's grades were dismissed earlier than their older brothers' classes; so Dan and Paul accompanied them to school each morning, but the girls walked home without them in the afternoon. Mama told them that if it ever happened to be raining when school let out that they could just ride the bus home.

"Look at those rain clouds rollin' in, Ellie-Belly," remarked Annie as they made their way to school one damp gray morning. "Now, don't forget. If it's raining this afternoon, we gotta ride the school bus home. Just meet me in front of the school where the buses park."

"OK, Sissy," replied Ellie. "Don't worry. I'll be there."

The girls soon parted ways and the school day began. Shortly before noon the rain began to fall in a steady downpour. Annie's attention wandered from the science book in front of her to the window where raindrops splashed and ran down the pane in little rivers.

*Yep, we're gonna be ridin' that ole bus this afternoon, for sure*, she thought as she listened to the rain pounding the roof overhead.

What Annie had not thought about, since she had never ridden a school bus before, was the fact that there was more than one school bus parked out front and they all traveled in different directions taking children home.

At the sound of the afternoon bell, Annie quickly gathered up her belongings and hurried out to meet Ellie. She spotted Ellie's white tow head as she stood among a group of first graders on the sidewalk near a long row of big yellow buses.

Annie hurried over and grabbed Ellie by the hand, and together they splish splashed across the wet sidewalk to the first bus in line. Up the narrow steps they climbed and sat down with a thump in the first empty seat they found. Ellie's damp hair clung to her forehead as she looked at Annie with a big grin on her face.

"Well, Sissy, you and me gonna have us a new adventure today, ain't we?"

"Yep, Ellie-Belly. And it starts right now," replied Annie as the bus's engine roared to life.

The girls giggled and held on to each other as the yellow bus bumped out of the school parking lot and onto the street. They each stared out the window at the rain, which showed no sign of letting up.

Suddenly a skinny boy in the seat across the aisle pointed his finger at Annie and Ellie and shouted, "Hey, who are you? You ain't supposed to be ridin' this bus. Hey, bus driver. These girls don't live on our route."

Annie and Ellie sat in stunned silence while the boy continued to announce to the whole busload of kids that they had a couple of stowaways hunkered down in seat number two. Only then did it occur to Annie that not just any bus would take them to their house out in the country.

Panic seized Annie as she heard a chorus of voices chanting, "Who are you? You don't belong on this bus!"

Quick as the lightning flashing overhead, Annie yanked Ellie up the aisle of the bus until she was standing just behind the driver.

"Let us off this bus, mister!" she demanded.

With a raised eyebrow and a shrug of his shoulders, the driver brought the bus to a stop and opened the squeaky door. Down the steps and out into the rain the girls fled, having no idea where they were or how they'd get home.

That day the little town of Draper seemed like a huge city to Annie and Ellie. Nothing looked familiar to either of them. Annie grabbed Ellie's hand and together they began walking up the street. Tears streamed down their cheeks as the rain pelted their heads. Annie had no idea which direction they should be going. Presently, a tall man wearing a long black raincoat stopped on the sidewalk and asked Annie what was wrong.

"We got on the wrong school bus, mister, and now we don't know where we are or how to get home," Annie sobbed.

"Well, don't cry about it," replied the man. Without another word, or even offering to help them, the man strode off down the street, leaving the girls clinging together in a panic. Once more they began trudging up the street in the rain.

"Ellie-Belly, I'll get us home. I don't know how just yet, but somehow I'll get us home," Annie promised, wiping her eyes and clutching Ellie's hand tightly.

Just then Annie spied a familiar face hurrying up the sidewalk toward them.

"Oh look, Ellie, it's Sarah!"

Sarah was an older girl who went to the same little church as Annie and Ellie.

"What in the world are you girls doing out here in the middle of town in this rainstorm by yourselves?" questioned Sarah.

Both girls began talking at once, trying to explain to Sarah how they'd gotten on the wrong bus at school. Once more Ellie burst into tears exclaiming, "And now, we don't know how to get home! We don't even know where home is." She sobbed, wiping her eyes with her wet sleeve.

"You poor babies," cooed Sarah gently. "I understand why you're so frightened. But don't worry. I'm here now, and I know exactly where you live. Just come with me and I'll see to it that you get home safe and sound."

By that time the sky had begun to lighten and the rain slowed to a gentle pitter patter as the girls followed Sarah across streets and out of the busy little town. Before long, Annie spotted a little white church in the distance, its slender cross steeple pointing toward a sky starting to show scattered patches of blue.

"There's our church, Sarah! I know where we are now. And I can get home from here!" Annie exclaimed happily.

"Are you sure?" asked Sarah. "Because I can take you all the way home if you want me to."

"No, Miss Sarah. I sure am glad you came along when you did. I don't know what me and Ellie would have done without your help. I ain't never been that scared a' anything in my whole borned days."

"Well, you're mighty welcome, girls. I am so glad I ran into you at just the right time. Now you're sure you'll be OK from here?"

"Oh yes, ma'am. We walk to church every Sunday. When I see that big cross I know I'm on the right road home. Besides, it's stopped raining now. Thank you, Miss Sarah. We'll see you next Sunday!"

Suddenly, Annie threw her wet arms around Sarah in a bear hug as Ellie followed suit. Sarah laughed and hugged them back, then turned with a wave and began heading back toward town.

"Ellie-Belly, I ain't gonna ride no bus ever again as long as I live. It can just rain on me all it wants to 'cause bein' wet's a whole lot better than bein' lost!"

With that the two girls skipped the rest of the way home, anxious to get into some dry clothes and tell Mama about the not-so-fun bus ride adventure.

That night a grateful Annie whispered quietly, "Dear God, thank you for sending Miss Sarah along when we needed help so bad." And as Mama sat in her chair by the fireplace mending a pair of Papa's socks, she heard Annie as she lay snuggled deep in her nice, dry bed softly humming that old hymn "The Way of the Cross Leads Home."

## CHAPTER 15

# Don't Tell about
# the Nails

Far sooner than Mama would have preferred, Papa was ready to move again, this time about thirty miles away to the city of Durham, North Carolina. Annie noticed the worried look on Mama's face that day as she began pulling out cardboard boxes to pack once again. Where in the world were they going to find the fifteen dollars they would have to pay the movers to get their belongings moved to the city?

Mama turned as Papa came banging in the door later that afternoon.

"Papa, I've decided to sell my sewing machine. We can use the money to pay the movers."

"You can't do that, Mama. What will you do when these girls need new dresses made?" Papa questioned.

"Well, there's no money to move us, and there sure ain't no money to buy material for new dresses. We'll just have to make do with what we have until we can do better. I'm gonna sell that machine and that's that!"

Annie knew that when Mama made up her mind about something there was no changing it. So, in no time at all the sewing machine was being carried out the front door by its happy new owner as Mama turned with a sigh. Annie didn't think Mama looked too happy as she addressed Papa.

"All right, Papa. Go find those movers," directed Mama, handing Papa the fifteen dollars she'd just collected.

When they moved to Durham Papa would be working at another cotton mill as a loom mechanic. When a problem caused one of the huge cotton looms to break down, Papa could take it completely apart, fix the problem and put it back together again.

However, work at the cotton mill was often unpredictable, and Papa knew that he could lose his job any time there was a slow-down in the workload. The price of cotton was like a pendulum, up one minute and down the next, always changing. The law of supply and demand affected the mill workers on a daily basis. All too often, the swing of the pendulum meant workers were losing their jobs and families were looking desperately for ways to feed hungry mouths and make ends meet.

Living in Durham was quite different from living out in the country. For one thing, the house Papa rented had a garage just a few steps from the house. Papa had never owned a car. Their transportation had always been a mule pulling a wagon when they lived out in the country. In the small town of Draper, Annie and her family had walked everywhere they went. So Papa had no real need for the garage that came with the house in the city.

The garage was built of wooden planks topped with a roof made of tin. And although Papa had no plans to use it, Annie and Ellie quickly discovered its potential as a terrific playhouse. Their playhouses had always been outdoors under a big shade tree if one was available. But now, shoot! They could play in the garage playhouse to their hearts' delight, even if it was raining cats and dogs outside.

The girls found themselves spending hours playing on the

dirt floor of that garage. Pasteboard boxes made their way into the garage to serve as tables. Small planks of wood supported by rocks made perfect shelves to store bakery items such as mud cakes and pies. Oh, yes! That garage was the perfect place for two little girls to while away the hours when Mama released them from their daily housekeeping chores.

However, their excitement with the newly acquired playhouse soon turned to dismay. It seemed that their next-door neighbor had his own plan for that garage. One evening Papa answered a knock on the front door to find Mr. Gunther standing on the front porch.

"Howdy, Albert," began Mr. Gunther in a friendly, neighborly greeting. "I noticed that you're not driving a car."

"No, no," answered Papa. "Never have owned a car myself."

"I see," Mr. Gunther replied. "In that case, I was wondering if perhaps you'd allow me to park my car in your garage for the time being?"

"Why, you just help yourself there, neighbor. Use it as long as you want to," Papa replied cheerfully.

Annie could hardly believe her ears! In a split second their playhouse had suddenly been jerked out from under them without so much as a "howdy do" from Papa. She and Ellie had spent many hours converting that vacant garage into their very own playhouse, arranging moss-covered beds in the bedrooms, building grocery shelves in the kitchen, and fixing up boxes of various sizes for tables and chests. And now, with a loud knock on their front door, all their hard work was about to be destroyed by a car that wasn't even theirs.

Annie dared not voice her opposition to what she'd just heard for fear she'd get a lickin' from Papa. After all, Papa knew little of Annie and Ellie's escapades in the little dirt floor shack, and Mama obviously felt no reason to inform him.

"Now where we gonna play, Annie?" moaned Ellie sadly later that evening. "We can't play in the garage with that ole car in there. They's not enough room. What we gonna do, Annie, huh? What we gonna do?" repeated Ellie.

"Hush up, Ellie-Belly. Let me do some thinkin' 'bout this. They's gotta be somethin' we can do to keep Mr. Gunther from usin' that garage. Just let me think on this a little while. Don't say a word to Papa and Mama 'bout none of this, you hear?"

"Yeah, Annie, I hear. But what we gonna do?"

The look on Annie's face told Ellie she'd better keep quiet

for a little while because Annie's brain was in thinkin' mode.

The next morning Annie and Ellie made their bed and washed the breakfast dishes in record time. Just as they dried the last dishes and placed them on the shelf they heard Mr. Gunther's car start up out in the garage.

"Gee whiz, Ellie-Belly. Ole Mr. Gunther sure didn't waste any time claiming that garage for his own, did he?" muttered Annie. "But that's OK. I've got us a surefire plan to take back what's ours. Now let's go see what all he's messed up."

The girls scurried across the yard and pulled on the big plank garage door. With a moan and a squeak the door swung open and sunlight spilled into the dark opening.

Ellie's mouth fell open at the sight of rocks scattered about amid clumps of green moss smashed flat. Pasteboard boxes lay in a crumpled heap near the front of the garage with several small wooden boards tossed hastily on top.

"Oh, Annie, what we gonna do?" began Ellie all over again.

"I'll tell you what we're gonna do, Ellie-Belly. We're gonna get our playhouse back. That's what we're gonna do. But you can't say a word to Mama or Papa 'bout this, or we'll both get killed. You hear me?"

"Oh no, Sissy. I ain't likin' the sound of this," wailed Ellie reluctantly.

"Hey, Ellie! If you want to get our playhouse back, you gotta trust me. Now here's what we gotta do."

Presently the two girls were busy picking up ruined mud pies, grocery shelves, and moss bed coverlets.

"Don't worry 'bout savin' any of this, Ellie-Belly. Just pile all of it over here in the corner. Our next playhouse will be better than this one ever was. Just you wait and see. I'll be right back."

While Ellie tossed the last bakery items on the pile in the corner, Annie ran outside and returned shortly with two limbs she'd broken off a nearby forsythia bush.

"Here, Ellie. We're gonna use these brooms to make the dirt on this ole garage floor smooth as a baby's behind. Now, git to smoothin'."

"But what are—" began Ellie.

"No time for questions, Ellie-Belly. Just do as I say. There's not a minute to waste."

Swirling clouds of dust rose from the dirt floor as each girl swished her broom back and forth from one side of the garage to the other. Soon Annie stood back to inspect their work.

"Good enough, Ellie. Now for the secret plan."

Annie reached swiftly into the pocket of her worn gingham dress and pulled out a handful of small, rusty nails.

"OK, Ellie. Me and you are gonna bury these nails in this ole dirt floor, right where Mr. Gunther's car tires roll in. Now, hurry up. Time's a'wastin'."

Ellie stood rooted to the spot with eyes as big as saucers just staring at Annie.

*Annie's really done it this time. We're gonna die when Mama and Papa find out about this.*

Annie saw Ellie's stricken face and tried to reassure her. "They ain't gonna find out, Ellie-Belly. That is, unless you tell them. Now we've had a lot of playhouses in our time, but if you tell our secret, this'll be the last one we'll ever have. 'Cause if Mama don't kill us dead, Papa will. So you'd better promise to keep this little secret inside that little head of yours, you got me?"

Ellie's blonde curls bobbed up and down as she stooped and began helping Annie stick the nails into the soft dirt, sharp point up.

"Now we'll just bury a few today, Ellie, and see what happens."

Soon the deed was done and the girls swung the garage door open. Ellie blinked as the bright sunlight spilled onto her face. Annie quietly closed the door to the garage and turned to follow Ellie into the house. Ellie surely hoped Annie's plan worked. Whether it worked or whether it failed, she knew she could never, ever tell a soul what they had done.

For the next few days, Annie and Ellie were busy with household chores. It seemed that Mama found more and more for them to do besides their usual dish washing and bed making. Not that it really mattered. Without their playhouse in the garage there wasn't much of a place outdoors to play without playing in the street. Annie and Ellie waited patiently for evidence that their scheme was working.

Annie had almost given up hope until early one morning she looked out the living room window and saw a red-faced Mr. Gunther down on his knees yanking at the right rear tire on his car. Off it came with a jerk, the force sending Mr. Gunther to the ground, flat on his behind. Annie raised her hand to cover the wide grin spreading rapidly across her face as she turned from the window.

"Just a matter of time," she whispered to herself. "Just a matter of time."

Annie and Ellie watched this scene repeat itself a second time, then a third over the course of the next two weeks. Neither girl entered the garage during that time except to replenish a nail here and there just in case the originals had somehow been buried too deep.

Papa and Mama had just stood up from the supper table one evening when there came another knock on the front door.

"Well, howdy, Gunther!" Annie and Ellie heard Papa exclaim loudly.

Ellie shot a quick look of alarm in Annie's direction, but Annie was staring at the floor, scarcely daring to breathe. Abruptly, Annie jumped up from the table and began stacking the dishes and carrying them to the kitchen without Mama even reminding her to do so. Ellie followed suit, all the while listening to the conversation coming from the front porch.

"Say you're havin' flat tires?" Annie heard Papa remark. "Well I declare, Gunther. What? You say you've had three already? Well, if that don't beat a hen a'peckin' in the woodpile."

Meanwhile, in the kitchen Annie was furiously splashing

soap suds around in the dishpan, anxious for the conversation on the front porch to end.

"You'll not be parkin' your car in the garage anymore, you say, Gunther? Well, now, I can't say as I blame you for that. Could be the people who lived here before had a workshop in that garage. Maybe that's where all them nails come from. I shore am sorry about that."

Ellie was rinsing as furiously as Annie was washing those dishes when they both heard the screen door squeak closed. Neither girl looked up from their dishpans as Papa's footsteps sounded behind them.

"What was that all about, Albert?" questioned Mama.

"Well, it seems that Gunther's been havin' flat tires on his automobile since he started parkin' down in the garage. Said he'd already changed three and he can't afford to lose another one, so he'll not be using the garage anymore."

"Annie!"

Annie felt sure the wild beating of her heart could be heard over the clatter of the dishes as she heard Papa call her name. Ellie was biting her lower lip as she placed the last of the dishes up on the shelf.

"Yes, Papa," answered Annie, trying to keep her voice from reflecting the fear she felt surging up inside her tummy.

"I know you and Ellie been playin' over in that garage barefoot. From now on, if you're gonna play in the garage, put your shoes on, so's you don't step on a rusty nail. Rusty nails and bare feet should never meet!"

"All right, Papa. We'll make sure we don't go in there ever again barefooted, will we, Ellie-Belly?"

"Sure won't, Papa. Not ever again, we promise."

That night as they lay on their bumpy straw-tick mattress the girls whispered about how they would design their new kitchen over in the playhouse. At last, their eyes began to droop and it was time to go to sleep. But neither Annie nor Ellie dared close their eyes without thanking the Lord above for a Papa who cared more about bare feet than flat tires.

# CHAPTER 16
## Hard Times

Annie knew that Papa and Mama had their hands full try-ing to feed the family and keep a roof over their heads. There was no place for a garden in the city, so everything they ate had to be purchased at the store. Cotton mill wages were not sufficient to cover housing and food for their family. One eve-ning Papa announced to Mama that he and Uncle Charlie had decided that it would make things easier if their two families moved in together. If they shared the rent maybe they could have more money for food.

Before long Annie was living elbow to elbow with her own family of six, plus Uncle Charlie's family of eight. Fourteen people crowded into a small house with a kitchen, dining room and two small bedrooms.

At first, Annie and Ellie were delighted to have their six cousins to play with during the day. At night it felt like they were having a giant sleepover with kids spread out all over the floor on pallet beds. Annie and Ellie had given up their straw-tick mattress bed to Aunt Lily and Uncle Charlie. The house was noisy during the day with sounds of children running and playing. Annie soon discovered that it was just about as noisy at night.

"Hey, Ellie-Belly." Annie nudged Ellie who was lying on the hard floor next to her. "Who's that snoring so loud? I can't sleep a wink. All that buzzin' sounds like a jar full of mad hornets. How's a body s'pose to sleep?"

"Beats me, Annie. Just stick your fingers in your ears."

"I tried that, Ellie. I got tired of holding my fingers in my ears. I'd rather hold a pillow over somebody's nose!"

"Oh, Sissy!" whispered Ellie. "How in the world would you figure out which nose to hold it over? They's too many kids piled up on this floor."

With that, Ellie turned over and wrapped her pillow over

her head and soon added her own little snuffle-snore to the symphony already in progress.

But not Annie. She had another problem. Her stomach added its own noise to the tumult. It had been a long time since supper and Annie had not eaten very much. In fact, with fourteen people in the house, the cornbread and milk and few potatoes Mama had fixed didn't go very far. Annie was not so sure this living arrangement Papa had worked out was such a good idea. Finally, sleep claimed Annie's eyes as she tossed and turned restlessly on the wooden floor.

A few days after the families moved in together a knock sounded on the front door.

"Somebody wants to talk to Aunt Lily," yelled Dan from the front door. "Somethin' 'bout a cookstove."

Mama and Papa had sold their family's cookstove when Aunt Lily and Uncle Charlie moved in. Aunt Lily had a brand-new stove and there was neither room nor a need to have two stoves in their small house. Besides, the money they got from the sale of the cookstove was money they could put on groceries.

Aunt Lily hurried to the door to find a young man dressed in a brown business suit.

"Good afternoon, ma'am," Annie heard the stranger begin. "I came to pick up a cookstove that you purchased some time ago and agreed to pay for on the installment plan. I have the sale papers right here, but so far we've received no money and no reply to our several requests for payment. Now I've come to pick up the stove unless you can make payment in full here today."

By that time all talking and playing inside the house had ceased as ten pairs of eyes were glued to the skinny man on the front porch waving some papers in his hand. Ten sets of ears listened carefully to see what Aunt Lily's reply would be.

"Well, sir, I'm sorry about missing the payments on the stove. You see, my husband's lost his job down at the cotton mill, and it's about more than we can do just to feed our kids. I hope to be able to make payment soon as he gets back to work if you can just wait a few more days."

"Well, I'm sorry too, ma'am. I really am. Lots of people are havin' a hard time these days. But the fact is, I have to take that stove back today if you can't pay for it."

With that, he turned and motioned for two men to join him. The men had been leaning up against a truck parked on the street, waiting for the signal to collect the stove for its return trip to the furniture store.

Ten pairs of eyes stared in disbelief as the two strode into the little house and began unhooking the stove from its attached pipes. Not a word was spoken until after men, pipes, and stove were out the door and on their way back to Reidsville, where Aunt Lily had purchased the stove on credit.

One by one, the kids, not knowing what to say about what had just happened, edged out the door into the yard to play.

Only the day before, Papa and Uncle Charlie had returned from work in the cotton mill, shoulders drooping as they entered the little house to tell Mama and Aunt Lily that the mill had laid off a group of workers, including the two of them. Once again, the pendulum had swung the wrong way and left men desperately searching for ways to feed their families.

Early the next morning, Papa made his way down to Harvey's General Store with a list of groceries Mama and Aunt Lily needed for the families. Later that afternoon, two delivery boys arrived with several boxes of food. Mama quickly made a place for them on the kitchen table. After placing the heavy boxes on the table the two boys turned to Papa expectantly.

"Oh, just put these groceries on my credit tab down at the store, boys. I'll be down to settle up the bill in a few days."

The boys looked at each other with worried expressions on their faces. Then the tall, blond-headed one spoke up hesitantly.

"We're sorry, Mr. Callahan. But Mr. Harvey won't let us extend credit on groceries no more. Too many people not payin' their bills, he says. If you can't pay us we don't have no choice but to take these groceries back to the store."

"But see here, boys. I've got a family to feed. I've always been good for my bills at Harvey's. Always paid every dime I owed."

"We don't mean you no harm, mister. But we've got our orders to collect payment upon delivery, and that's what we gotta do."

Annie realized for the second time that week that her family was struggling to survive. First, Papa and Uncle Charlie had both lost their jobs on the same day. Then Aunt Lily lost her cookstove, and now these boys were loading up their groceries to haul back to the store. What in the world would they do with fourteen people in the house, no money for food, and no stove to cook food on if they had any?

Suddenly, her thoughts were interrupted by the bang of the

front gate. Mrs. Gilliam from across the street was hurrying up the sidewalk to the door.

"Hey there, Annie. Is your Mama inside?"

"Yes, ma'am. She sure is," replied Annie, opening the door. "I think she's in the kitchen."

"Wonder what she wants, Sissy?" questioned Ellie as Mrs. Gilliam disappeared into the house.

"Let's go see, Ellie-Belly."

The girls ran into the kitchen just in time to hear Mrs. Gilliam say, "Oh, that's wonderful. I'm so glad you can use all that food I cooked up. I don't know why my company didn't show up today as I expected. But land sakes! Me and Robert can't eat all that stuff, and we sure can't let it go to waste. Send a couple of the boys over with me to get it."

Mama and Aunt Lily looked like the weight of the world had been lifted off their shoulders as they sent Dan and Paul across the street with little Mrs. Gilliam leading the way.

What a feast the family had that night! By the time Mama and Aunt Lily had the boxes emptied, there were steaming bowls of chicken, mashed potatoes, green beans, corn, and big fluffy biscuits piled high on a platter.

Fourteen hungry people gathered around the table as Papa lifted his voice in humble prayer thanking God for Mrs. Gilliam who had blessed them with all that food.

Somehow, the floor didn't seem quite so hard to Annie that night, nor the snoring quite so loud. With a grateful heart and a full tummy Annie thanked the Lord for little Mrs. Gilliam across the street.

"Dear God," Annie whispered into the darkness. "I wonder did Mrs. Gilliam just pretend she had company that didn't show up so's she could bring us all that food? She shorely must be an angel."

## CHAPTER 17

# Trouble in the Amen Corner

The only time Annie and Ellie ever got any toys was at Christmas. Then they would get a fifty-cent doll, a twenty-five-cent tea set and maybe a ten-cent bouncy ball. Both girls were delighted with these small gifts to entertain them for days to come. However, since Papa was searching for work and finding little, there was no money for toys.

A few days before Christmas Mama dug around in her sewing box and found a pretty scrap of pink checked material. She hid the cloth until the girls had gone to sleep. Then she began stitching little dresses with bonnets to match for the girls' old dolls. If they couldn't have new dolls at least they would have new outfits to dress the old ones in.

Annie and Ellie were thrilled on Christmas morning when they saw the new doll clothes that Mama had stitched by hand while they were fast asleep. In fact, once the dolls were dressed up in their brand-new attire they looked almost like new.

"Shucks, Ellie. These dolls are dressed up in their Sunday-go-to-meetin' dresses and that's just where we're gonna take them," declared Annie.

Annie's family had not attended church much in recent days because, to tell the truth, they didn't have decent clothes to wear out in public. Everyone was wearing patched clothes, some with patches on top of patches. So their churchgoing had suffered as a result.

But Annie and Ellie had been to church enough to remember about how a church service should be conducted. So at Annie's suggestion the children all trooped downstairs to the basement to begin Sunday worship.

Annie, Ellie, their two brothers and all the cousins began busily transforming the basement into a church. Dan and Paul found two planks and laid them across chairs to make benches to seat the congregation. Annie and Ellie found a smaller bench to serve as the mourners' bench, or the altar. A tall cardboard box made the perfect pulpit. Soon it was time for the service to begin.

"Lloyd, you're gonna be preachin' today. Dolly and Lois, you two can lead the singin'," directed Annie as she and the others sat down on their plank pews ready to begin worship.

"She'll be comin' 'round the mountain when she comes!" belted out Dolly.

"She'll be comin' 'round the mountain when she comes!" joined in Lois, at the top of her lungs.

Annie looked over at Ellie who was staring in astonishment at her two singing cousins.

"Hey!" Ellie jumped to her feet, nearly knocking the plank pew off its foundation. "You know that ain't no church song!"

With that the two choir leaders broke into peals of laughter.

"Oh, we're just funnin' you, Ellie! We know that ain't no church song," laughed Dolly.

"Just keep yer britches on, everybody. This here next song is a for sure church song," promised Lois.

"OK, and this time you just remember where you are, young ladies!" reminded Annie.

Soon the air was filled with strains of "Amazing Grace, How Sweet the Sound."

"Now that's more like it," agreed Annie.

The rest of the congregation joined in heartily until the last verse ended. Then they all sat back down as Lloyd assumed his position at the pulpit for the sermon to begin.

And what a sermon it was! Lloyd took his calling very seriously, and was soon admonishing his audience to quit their wicked ways and repent before the devil took them all to a place where it was very hot and there would be no water to quench their scorching tongues!

As his sermon came to a close, he called for anyone who wanted to go to heaven instead of that other hot place to come forward for prayer. Quickly the mourners' bench was filled with mourners, all busy repenting for their wickedness.

What rejoicing there was in the basement that day as the sinners confessed their sins, then jumped to their feet to shout the victory!

Unfortunately, Aunt Lily, a very religious woman who knew all about repenting and shouting, descended the basement steps to see what all the commotion was about.

Shouts of "Praise the Lord!" and "Hallelujah!" met her ears as she stared in wonder at the scene below. Soon her own shouts were added to the tumult. Only her shouts were not shouts of rejoicing.

"What on earth are you children doing?" she demanded indignantly.

Aunt Lily had the mistaken idea that the children were making fun of how they'd seen her worship and praise the Lord, even around the house.

"Oh, Mother," explained Dolly. "We're just playin' church down here. You can come help us out if you want to."

"I'll do no such thing, little missy. And you'll not be pretending to have church in this basement ever again. You should be ashamed of yourselves, the whole lot of you. Now get up here, all of you! And don't ever let me hear you mocking what goes on down at the church no more! Do you hear me?"

"Yes, ma'am," answered a chorus of confused voices from below.

Reluctantly, the children began to dismantle their church, and soon the benches, altar, and pulpit were once more just ordinary boards and cardboard boxes taking up room in the damp basement.

"I sure am glad, dear God," Annie whispered later that night as she lay on the floor beside her sleeping cousins, "that you know we didn't mean no harm. Please help Aunt Lily understand it too. By the way. Lloyd's a pretty good preacher, ain't he, God?"

# CHAPTER 18
## *Elbow Room*

Annie quickly decided that having fourteen people in a four-room house was not very much fun after all. There was no room to turn around without bumping into someone. It seemed there was a child or an adult stuck in every nook and cranny. And there weren't that many nooks and crannies.

"A'body ain't even got room to sneeze around here," muttered Annie to herself crossly.

Even mealtime was not a sit-down affair. There was standing room only while everyone ate what little food Papa and Uncle Charlie had worked or bartered for.

At first, it had been fun having six more playmates around

every day. But lately, it seemed all they did was argue about what game they would play or whose turn it was. Annie was tired of all the fussing and bickering that happened when ten kids all wanted their way at once. Whew! It was a dadgum nightmare sometimes. Annie began to wish desperately that her family could have their own house again where she could play with Ellie all by herself.

*Oh happy day!* thought Annie when Papa came in one afternoon with those oh so familiar words.

"Pack up, Mama! We're movin' back to the country."

"Where we movin', Papa?" questioned Ellie curiously. She thought they'd already lived in every place there was out in the country.

"I found a house for us to rent out on Cornwallis Road, Little Bit. I can find a little work helping some of the neighboring farmers out there. Now you and Annie help Mama pack our duds and get ready to head on out."

In the shake of a sheep's tail, Annie flew in helping Mama find pasteboard boxes to pack up their few belongings once again.

Soon they were hearing the clip clop of horses' hooves up ahead of the rickety old farm wagon Papa had borrowed to haul the family just a little way out of town to the house on Corn-wallis Road. Behind them, eight pairs of hands waved goodbye as they left Uncle Charlie and his family behind. Annie noticed the look of relief on Aunt Lily's face when the wagon with its occupants rolled out into the street. After spending three weeks in a house with wall-to-wall people, Annie felt sure that Aunt Lily had probably been down in the basement having a prayer meeting of her own, asking the Lord to please see fit to meet the two families' needs with different living arrangements.

"Who knows?" mused Annie. "Aunt Lily is probably dancin' around that little ole house right now, a'shoutin' the victory for answered prayer."

Annie felt like doing a little shouting of her own as the horses clip clopped along, hauling her family past fields of sweet potatoes, black-eyed peas, and peanuts. It was late sum-mer and the farmers along Cornwallis Road would soon begin harvesting those crops.

Annie breathed in great gulps of fresh air and sunshine as the wagon creaked along the dusty road.

"Whoa!" Papa hollered as he finally drew the horses up to a small frame house a few hundred yards off the road.

Down from the dusty wagon scrambled Annie and Ellie, anxious once more to investigate their new surroundings.

"Not so fast, girls," Mama called. "There's unpacking to be done before you can play. Now, grab a box and head into the house."

Reluctantly, Annie and Ellie returned to the wagon to help Mama unload. As soon as everything was unpacked, Papa showed the girls where the well was located. The water buckets would need to be filled with fresh water before Mama started cooking supper.

Finally, Mama finished stuffing fresh straw into the last straw-tick mattress and turned with a sigh.

"Girls, there'll not be much cookin' going on tonight. I'm pleased as punch to see this old cookstove sitting here in the kitchen. But I shore am tired from packin' and unpackin' and stuffing these straw ticks. We'll just have us a big pone of cornbread and some milk for supper. Won't take long to get the cornbread baked, so you two have some time to frolic about outdoors before suppertime. Just mind you stay in sight of the house and don't go gettin' yourselves lost."

"We will, and we won't!" promised the girls.

Although the little house on Cornwallis Road was only a few miles out of town, Annie and Ellie were once again enjoying the feel of the country. The summer sun warmed their faces as they stood gazing at the large fields of cotton, peanuts, and sweet potatoes which all but surrounded their house. Papa and the boys would be working long hours in these fields helping other tenant farmers harvest the crops in exchange for food for the family, along with what meager wage the land owner could afford to pay. It was usually fifty cents each for a ten-hour day.

"Now boys," Papa advised. "I know it's not easy workin' ten hours a day in the field with the hot sun beatin' down on our heads. And I know we're only makin' fifty cents for a day's work. But we all know we can't make it livin' in town in a four-room house, tryin' to feed fourteen people. It just didn't work out."

"Yes, Papa," Dan agreed. "Diggin' all 'em taters and pickin' cotton shore ain't much fun. But livin' with all 'em cousins in that little ole house wasn't much fun either."

Little did Annie and Ellie realize that they too, along with the rest of the family, would soon be pulling up peanut vines, scratching in the ground for sweet potatoes, and dragging a bag through a field of cotton to help keep their family fed.

## CHAPTER 19

# A Sneaky Snake and a Great Escape

"It sure was nice sleepin' in our own bed last night," exclaimed Annie as she and Ellie smoothed the straw tick into place the next morning.

"Yeah," giggled Ellie. "I only heard three people snorin' before I fell asleep."

What a relief it was to wake up to only six people in the house instead of fourteen. Although Annie loved her cousins, she hoped and prayed they would never have to share a house again.

Once the girls had carried buckets of fresh water into the kitchen from the well out back, their morning chores were finished.

"Hey, Ellie-Belly! How's about me and you goin' on a little ole picnic? It's a sun-washed day, just right for some explorin'."

Before Annie finished speaking, Ellie grabbed her small tin lard bucket off the wooden peg in the kitchen, eager to fill it with a picnic lunch and be off on another adventure. Presently a frown puckered her face as she turned to Annie.

"Annie, we don't have nothin' to eat for no picnic. How can we have a picnic with nothin' to put in our bucket? Nope, we just can't go on no picnic today."

"Oh yes we can," countered Annie. "See, right here's two boiled taters left from breakfast this mornin'. And 'sides all that, I saw a grapevine over yonder at the edge of the yard last night jus' hangin' full of big ole juicy grapes. Boiled taters and grapes. Why that's a picnic fit for a king."

*Annie always has a way of figurin' things out,* smiled Ellie to herself.

Plunk! Plunk! Went two boiled potatoes into the tin bucket, and soon the girls were skipping merrily toward the waiting grapevines, swinging their picnic bucket between them with the two boiled potatoes bumping around inside, thumpity-thump.

The leafy green grapevines draped across a wooden trellis and spilled over the ends, partially hiding a set of wooden posts that supported the structure. The grapes hung in juicy clusters just out of reach of the girls' outstretched hands. Try as they may, even standing on tippy toes, the girls could not quite reach the beckoning treasures.

"Oh, phooey, Annie. Now we just got boiled taters for our picnic. That's not much of a picnic if you ask me," whined Ellie.

"Well, I don't 'member askin' you. Have you forgot how I used to climb up the side of the chicken house out on Eggleton Farm? Climbin' up this lil' ole grapevine ain't nothin'. Now you just stand right here under the trellis and hold up the bucket. I'm gonna climb up there and grab a big bunch of grapes and drop them right in there. Now you just stand right over here like I told you."

Annie pointed to a spot directly under a tangle of cascading green leaves. Ellie moved obediently to the place where Annie was pointing.

In a flash, Annie was skinning up the wooden post, brushing away the curling vines that clung to her arms and stuck to her dress.

"Get ready, Ellie," shouted Annie as she reached the top.

Holding on to the wooden trellis with one hand, Annie stretched herself out over the grapevines as far as she could, grasping for the huge cluster of purple sweetness barely within her reach.

Suddenly, she found herself staring eye to eye with a long green garden snake, its cleverly camouflaged body curled around the top rungs of the trellis, tongue flicking out, daring Annie to touch the juicy fruit at her fingertips.

"Snake!" screamed Annie as she tumbled backward down the rough wooden post and landed in a frightened heap on the ground.

Ellie stood frozen to the spot under the trellis, their tin bucket dangling loosely in her trembling hand.

Annie sprang to her feet just long enough to jerk Ellie away from the slithering guardian of the grapevines before collapsing on the grass to catch her breath.

"Well, Ellie-Belly," Annie gasped when she finally found her voice. "I think two boiled taters will make a fine picnic lunch. I don't aim to fight no snake for the biggest cluster of grapes on that whole dadgum grapevine."

Just then the girls heard Mama holler from the front porch.

"Come on back to the house, girls. We've got an errand to run."

Breathlessly, the girls made their way back to the front porch, all hopes of a picnic forgotten for that day.

## CHAPTER 20

# No Rabbit Stew
# Tonight

"Girls, we're gonna go check those rabbit traps Papa and the boys set out and baited last night," declared Mama when the girls arrived on the front porch. "Sure would be nice to have some fresh meat to cook for a change to go with them taters."

Annie could not remember the last time the family had meat of any kind to eat. When they lived out on Eggleton Farm they had chickens that sometimes ended up in a big pot on Mama's cookstove. But in town there were no chickens to be had; or at least there had been no money to buy them. So a trip to the rabbit gum seemed like a great idea to Annie.

*I don't know what rabbit stew tastes like*, Annie thought to herself. *But it shore will beat goin' to bed with that hungry feelin' gnawin' at my tummy tonight.* So off the trio trudged across the pasture to the rabbit traps.

Papa and the boys were working down below the house cutting cord wood for Mr. Roberts.

"Looky yonder, Mama!" Ellie squealed with delight as they neared the large wooden trap. "They's a rabbit in there, Mama! We caught one!"

Annie laughed as Ellie danced circles around Mama, stopping only long enough to peer at the door of the rabbit trap, which had slammed closed when the unsuspecting rabbit had followed the bait trail inside, tripping the string that held the trap door open.

Mama pushed her gingham dress tail to one side as she knelt down on the dusty ground in front of the trap door.

"I'll get this feller outta this trap and take him down to Papa," declared Mama. "He can clean it and get it ready for rabbit stew."

Annie and Ellie stared in amazement as Mama carefully lifted the trap door, reached inside and brought out a big brown ball of fur, squirming and kicking its legs like a wind-mill in a tornado.

Annie was laughing so hard she could hardly breathe as Mama started off down through the field toward Papa, hang-ing on to that big rabbit's hind legs, while the front two legs plowed the air in a desperate attempt to break free.

Ellie stood watching, her mouth hanging open in shock. Then, she too burst into peals of laughter as she watched that frightened rabbit try to escape.

Papa stopped working when he saw Mama approaching with that huge rabbit in tow.

Suddenly, with a loud squeal, a gigantic kick, and a fran-tic forward lunge, the rabbit jerked free of Mama's grasp and sprang to the ground. Off it scampered straight into the near-by woods, leaving Mama staring after it, scratched and emp-ty-handed.

For a few seconds all was silent as Annie's family watched their supper make its hasty getaway. All at once, great shouts of laughter filled the afternoon air, but this time it was not coming from Annie or Ellie. Papa stood with his head thrown back, his tummy shaking like a bowl of Jell-O. Presently,

Mama joined Papa, tears of laughter streaming down her own flushed cheeks.

"Well, Papa," chuckled Mama when she finally stopped for breath. "We may have rabbit stew for supper, but it won't be tonight's supper."

"Come on, girls. Let's head back to the house. We've got taters to boil."

# CHAPTER 21
## Goats Gotta Eat Too!

Annie trudged wearily up the road heading home from the sweet potato patch where she and her family had worked all day. Mr. Meadows, a neighboring farmer, had plowed up a big field of sweet potatoes and harvested them. But there were a few left in the ground.

"If you'll go through and dig out what's left in the ground, you can have half of them," Mr. Meadows had promised Papa.

Somewhere in the back of her mind Annie remembered Mama reading a story from the Bible about a lady named Ruth who gathered grain the reapers had left behind.

*Seems to me like she got to keep all she found,* pondered Annie. *And I bet she found more grain than we'll find sweet taters.*

The next morning Papa led the whole family down the road to the sweet potato patch where they spent the day digging and scratching around for the few hidden vegetables.

It had been the same with a field of peanuts a few days earlier. Annie and Ellie had both learned how to pull the peanut vines up out of the sandy loam soil, shake the loose dirt off, and turn them upside down to dry in the sun. When the peanuts were gathered, not every shell had nuts inside. Because of the long growing season in the eastern part of North Carolina where they lived, the peanut vines kept blooming right up until harvest. When the vines were ready to pull, the late blooming pods had not had time to mature properly, so the peanut shell would often be empty. These hollow shells were called "pops." Again, Annie's family was allowed to keep only half of what they scratched out of the ground, pops included.

Another day they had all gathered black-eyed peas, taking half of what they picked home with them. And even though Annie hated giving up playtime with Ellie, it was their responsibility to help put food on the table and she dared not complain. At least, not out loud.

What Annie hated most of all was picking cotton. You couldn't eat cotton, but Mr. Meadows paid them in real money; a whopping penny a pound. Mama would make sure Annie and Ellie tied on their cotton sunbonnets in the mornings before they left for the field. The gathered ruffle at the back of the bonnet kept the sun off their necks, and the wide brim on the front helped to shelter their faces from the sun's hot rays. Once they got to the field, each girl was given a big sack with a strap that fit over her shoulder.

Annie liked to feel the clumps of soft cotton in her hands. What she did not like, however, was constantly getting pricked by the sharp edges of the boll that held that softness. You could not use gloves to pick cotton, and by the end of the day both Annie's and Ellie's hands would be sore and often bleeding from all the sticks and pricks. Annie thought it was an awful lot of hard work for so little pay. But again, she held her tongue, realizing the rest of her family was just as sore and tired as she was.

One afternoon as Annie neared the house after a long muggy day of picking cotton, she heard an awful commotion coming from inside.

Bang! Clatter! Crash! Came the noises as Annie rushed

through the front door. Whatever, or whoever it was, was in her and Ellie's bedroom. Annie burst through the bedroom door to find the neighbor's two goats, Daisy and Lily Belle, trampling around on top of her bed, pulling straw out of the straw-tick mattress and chewing away.

"What in the tarnation are you doin'?" screamed Annie, waving her arms to shoo the goats off the bed. "Get outta here! Shoo! Go!"

Mama and Ellie arrived in the front yard just in time to see two frightened goats come flying out the front door of their house with Annie in hot pursuit.

"Land sakes! What's goin' on here?" Mama squawked, watching the two goats fleeing from a broom-wielding Annie.

"Seems Daisy and Lily Belle paid us a visit while we were in the cotton field," replied Annie. "And pert near ate mine and Ellie's bed up!"

A trail of straw led Mama and Ellie to the scene of the goats' mischief. Apparently the goats, noting the absence of a screen door to deter them, had wandered into the house and made themselves at home while the occupants worked in the cotton field.

"I guess that's what we get for leaving the door standin' open," sighed Mama as she bent down to gather up the trail of straw.

After a quick supper of cornbread and cold, sweet milk, Annie and Ellie swept up the scattered clumps of straw and shoved them back into the straw-tick mattress, smoothing out the lumps as best they could before crawling wearily into bed.

When Annie's head hit the pillow, her mouth turned up in a half grin as she pictured Daisy and Lily Belle standing in the middle of her bed, munching away on the straw.

"Well, I guess goats get hungry too, don't they, God?"

But before God had time to answer, Annie was sound asleep.

# CHAPTER 22
## A Sticky Situation

By and by all the summer crops had been gathered and there was no more work to be done in the fields. A cool nip in the morning air whispered warnings of colder days just ahead. Annie watched the school bus rumble by each morning filled with chattering children on their way to the school in town. Neither Mama nor Papa had mentioned a word to Annie or her siblings about returning to school.

Annie looked down at her patched and faded dress Mama had made out of a flour sack. Her knees peeked out from beneath the hem, which had once covered her legs halfway down. Luckily, she was "as skinny as a rail fence" as her brothers teased her, so the dress still fit her slender body. She was wearing the best she had, and Ellie fared no better.

Annie remembered how Mama had sold her sewing machine to get the money to pay a man with a truck to move them from Draper to Durham, one of the many places they'd lived over the last few years. Even if she still had the machine, there was no money to buy material for new school clothes. And so Annie watched silently as the big yellow bus clattered by each morning on its appointed route, leaving a cloud of dust and a somber Annie in its wake.

Annie didn't really miss going to school that much. She never really felt like she belonged there anyway. She was already older than most of the other kids in her grade. Papa and Mama had not felt it necessary to start her in school until she was already eight years old. By then the children her age were in second grade and she was stuck in first. Being tall for her age didn't help matters either. She knew she stuck out like a big sore thumb.

One thing Annie did miss was being able to check out library books to bring home and read. Oh, how she did love to read! Books were like good friends who stayed with you and kept you company even when you were alone. Papa and Mama could read, but neither of them loved to read like Annie did, so it didn't seem all that important to them to have books around the house.

Annie wondered why nobody from school had come to see why four children out on Cornwallis Road had not returned to school that fall. Not the principal, not a teacher, not even the truant officer paid a visit to inquire about the children's absence.

"Maybe that ole school's so crowded they don't even know we're not there," Annie decided.

However, Annie was not one to dwell on things she could not have or couldn't change. Fortunately, her creative imagination provided Ellie and her with hours of fun, and they were seldom bored.

Such was the case one frosty morning in October. Goldenrods nodded their fuzzy yellow heads as a gentle morning breeze rippled through the big pasture behind the house.

"Grab your coat, Ellie-Belly," ordered Annie as she stuck her arms through the too-short sleeves of her own winter jacket. "See them goldenrods bloomin' over in the pasture? They look like big globs of yellow butter, melting and running down the stem. Wouldn't a big bouquet of them things look awful purty on Mama's kitchen table, Ellie?"

Ellie slid her arms quickly through her own jacket and ran to join Annie who was already on her way to the pasture.

"I know where they's a big jar we can put our bouquet in, Annie," offered Ellie excitedly.

Over the pasture the girls romped, breaking clusters of powdery sunshine from their long green stems. Neither girl had given the slightest attention to the stiff, stubby cocklebur plants growing in profusion alongside the goldenrods until Annie looked down at her coat.

"Oh, my goodness!"

Clinging fast to the wool coat were dozens of thumb-sized burs, looking to Annie very much like little bitty porcupine eggs.

Throwing aside her armload of goldenrod blooms, Annie began to frolic back and forth through the pasture, her coat gathering dozens more of the sticky burs with each trip. Ellie soon forgot her own bouquet and followed Annie's lead.

"Bet I can pick up more passengers than you!" Annie yelled over her shoulder.

It was not long before the girls' coats were one big mass of sharp, sticky cockleburs. And to think, all they had to do was run through the pasture to collect all these funny little stowaways.

"I bet nobody else around here has a coat made out of porky pine burs," laughed Ellie. "Let's go show Mama. She'll think we look so funny in our new winter coats."

With their goldenrod bouquets long forgotten, the girls hurried back to the house to show Mama their new discovery.

"What in thunder have you girls done?" she shouted, staring in dismay at the dozens of cockleburs clinging to each girl's coat.

Suddenly, having the only porcupine coat in the neighborhood didn't seem like such a good idea to Ellie, or to Annie.

"You girls just set your little selves right down on this front porch and start pickin' them pesky burs off your coats. And don't you stop until you've pulled every cotton-pickin' one of them things off. Now, git to it! You'll soon find out why folks around here call them burs the devil's pin cushion!"

Annie and Ellie quickly discovered that getting the cockleburs off their coats was a heck of a lot harder than putting them on. The sun was slipping below the horizon by the time the last bur was pulled loose.

Mama had little mercy on the girls' discomfort as they plunged sore, pricked fingers into the waiting dishwater after supper. Their fingers stung like fire in the hot, soapy water.

Finally, their task completed, they emptied the water, dried their reddened hands, and pulled their nightgowns over sleepy heads. Ellie crawled into bed beside Annie with a long sigh.

"Annie," she muttered wearily. "Do you think you could find us somethin' to do tomorrow that don't involve the devil?"

## CHAPTER 23
# *The Letter*

Winter winds were howling around the corners of the little frame house on Cornwallis Road much too soon for Annie's liking. Being stuck inside was not her idea of fun. She was most happy when she and Ellie could traipse around and about the farm in the sunshine. But the frigid winter wind held the girls hostage inside the farmhouse, daring them to poke their noses out the door.

Papa and the boys spent most of their time over in the barn these days, tending the animals, mending a broken harness here, sharpening a plow blade there, in preparation for the spring planting season.

But they weren't the only ones mending things. Mama's lap was always filled to overflowing with a pile of overalls, waiting to be mended. It was a challenge to sew new patches on overalls that had been patched so many times before.

Winter brought challenges for the girls as well. Annie and Ellie were not ones to sit still for very long at a time. Annie had some figuring out of her own to do, and it wasn't long until she had a plan up her sleeve.

"Ellie, bring that lazy ole ball of fur over here to me," ordered Annie, pointing to the large tabby cat curled up contentedly on the fireplace hearth. "I'm thinkin' she needs a little exercise."

Over to the hearth skipped Ellie, scooping up a startled tabby cat to deposit into Annie's waiting lap.

"Now, you hold her still, Ellie-Belly, while I put on her ballet slippers."

Tabby lay squirming in Annie's lap while she quickly tied fuzzy white socks onto each furry paw. Just as she tied the last sock in place, Tabby sprang from her resting place to the floor below.

"Let the dancing begin!" yelled Annie.

And such dancing there was as Tabby jumped and pawed, scratched and clawed, all in a frantic effort to get those pesky booties off her feet. What a funny sight to behold! Around the table and across the kitchen floor Tabby flew, slipping and sliding and tumbling around, stopping only long enough to bite and pull desperately at her dancing slippers.

"Annie, you shouldn't be tormentin' that poor ole cat. She was just mindin' her own business 'til you disturbed her nap by the fire," scolded Mama. But Annie had already seen Mama chuckling as she watched Tabby scampering around the room in her sock feet.

Suddenly the kitchen door burst open with a swoosh as Papa entered, huffing and puffing and stomping his boots.

"Get over here by the fire and warm yourself, Papa. Your nose is as red as a pickled beet."

Mama hurried to the kitchen to bring Papa a hot cup of coffee from the pot she kept warming on the old cookstove.

About that time Tabby came racing back around the table, dashed through Papa's legs and collapsed on the floor to launch another attack on her booties.

"Bet I can guess whose idea that was," laughed Papa as he

watched the flustered cat struggling to free herself, one paw at a time.

"A'body's gotta think up somethin' to do when it's too cold to go outside, Papa. Ain't she funny, Papa? Ain't she the funniest thang you ever saw?" questioned Annie gleefully.

With all the laughter and commotion going on, nobody had noticed the letter Papa was holding in his hand until he spoke.

"Mailman just dropped off this here letter from Granddaddy up in the mountains."

"Oh, no! Granddaddy ain't never been much of a one to write letters. Ain't nobody sick up there, is they?" worried Mama.

"No, no. Everybody's fine," replied Papa. "He just says he's as lonesome as a hoot owl in the dark of night with all of us down here in the flatlands. Says he'd be pleased as pie for us to come live with him up in the mountains."

Ellie looked at Annie, her eyes as big as saucers. Annie's mouth dropped open as she stared at Papa, soaking in every word.

Annie had missed Granddaddy too. She missed his twinkling blue eyes and his deep rumbling laughter, and especially the funny stories he told when he came to visit. The mountains seemed so very far away.

"How we gonna get all the way up to Mars Hill, Papa? All we got to travel in is an old farm wagon. Wouldn't that be a sight to behold; all six of us piled into that old wagon with a mule a'pullin' us up Old Fort Mountain. 'Sides all that, it ain't even our wagon and he ain't even our mule," declared Mama.

"Granddaddy's already got that figgered out," Papa replied. "He's gonna borry a big truck from a friend of his. Big enough to haul us and what belongings we have to the mountains, he says. I don't know. I just don't know. But I do know one thing. They's a cow or two out in the barn a'waitin' to be milked and I gotta get out there and milk 'em."

With that, Papa set his coffee cup down, laid Granddaddy's letter on the table beside it and hurried back out the kitchen door to the barn.

Mama went back to her mending without a word, but Annie noticed that every few minutes her needle would stop moving and she would be staring into the flickering fireplace, deep in thought.

Annie found it hard to fall asleep that night. Long after Ellie's snuffle-snore sounded beside her she was still wide awake, staring into the darkness as dozens of questions popped into her head.

*Why did Granddaddy move away from us up to them mountains in the first place?*

Annie had never known her grandmother. She died before Annie was born.

*Did Granddaddy move to get away from sad memories? What would it be like, livin' there?*

Annie had seen postcards with pictures of beautiful blue mountain ranges rising in rippled peaks, which seemed to touch the sky above.

*Is it really true that cows in the mountains have two short legs and two long legs, so's they can stand on them hillsides without fallin' over? That's what Granddaddy said. And Granddaddy shore knows a lot about things in the mountains.*

The fire crackled and popped, its flames dancing in the stone fireplace far into the night while Papa and Mama discussed the move to the mountains. Finally, the last log burned through and dropped with a thud and a sizzle to join the smoldering coals below.

"That settles it then, Mama. I'll write back and tell Granddaddy to come on down and get us in time for spring plantin'. Me and the boys will help him plant a big garden that we won't have to share with nobody. I'll find work around there some-where, helpin' some of the other farmers out. The good Lord'll take care of us and we'll be all right. Yessiree! We'll be all right," declared Papa.

# CHAPTER 24

# Farewell to the Flatlands

"Ellie-Belly, we're finally gonna get to see them funny-lookin' cows!" squealed Annie as soon as she heard the news the next day. "You know, the ones Granddaddy said have two long legs and two short ones so's they can walk around the sides of them mountains?"

Dan stood up from the table where he'd just polished off a big helping of biscuits and gravy.

"Annie, you knucklehead. Ain't no cow nowhere got two short legs and two long ones."

"You ain't never been to the mountains, Dan," barked Annie. "You don't know nothin' 'bout the mountains."

"I don't know nothin' 'bout no mountains, Annie. But I do know a thang or two about cows. That's just another one of Granddaddy's tall tales."

"Enough of this talk about cows!" Mama scolded. "Now, Dan, if you know so much about cows, you'll know they's two out in the barn right now bawlin' their heads off, waitin' to be fed."

Quickly, Dan pulled on his worn winter coat and headed out to the barn, banging the kitchen door closed behind him, but not before sticking his tongue out at Annie who sat at the table, dipping her biscuit into a hot plate of gravy.

The days following Papa's decision seemed especially long. Annie and Ellie could hardly wait for spring to come. Mama tried to keep them occupied with inside fun after their morning chores were finished. She showed them how to fold a paper bag to cut out paper dolls, so that when you unfolded the paper all the dolls were holding hands in one long, unbroken line. She made it look so easy. But as hard as Annie tried to make her dolls look like Mama's, there was always one doll that had a mind of its own and wouldn't hold hands with the next one in line.

"My dolls don't wanna hold hands," complained Annie. "Come on, Ellie. Let's you and me go down to the barn and poke around for a while."

"You girls put on your coats and 'boggans first. And mind that you don't get in the boys' or Papa's way down there," called Mama.

Annie and Ellie had discovered that not much happened on Cornwallis Road in the dead of winter. So even a trip to the barn to poke around in the hayloft was better than being indoors all day. Mama said all that would change once they moved to the mountains. The children would all be back in school next year. Annie was not sure how she felt about that. *How in the world will we ever catch up?* she wondered silently.

"Oh well, no need to cross that bridge 'til we come to it," she whispered to herself.

Off to the barn the girls scampered, eager to find anything of interest they may have missed on their last visit. The old log barn was covered with moss. Cobwebs clung to the edges of ragged shingles, and last year's wasp nests dotted the eaves underneath. Still, there was a certain magic about the old struc-ture that drew the girls inside.

Maybe it was the hayloft with its mound of soft yellow hay. The girls had been known to climb up the wooden ladder and jump up and down in the middle of the scratchy haystack. That is, until the boys started complaining to Papa about having to gather up the loose hay that rained down from the loft with each bounce and plop.

This morning, Papa and the boys were working at the grinding wheel, sharpening farm tools for spring planting. The job took two people, one to hold the blade against the grindstone and the other to turn the wheel. Papa bought the stone to make the grindstone wheel from a peddler making his rounds back in the late fall, and now it was being put to good use.

Annie and Ellie watched sparks fly as Papa held one tool after another up to the noisy wheel. Annie couldn't quite understand why they were going to the trouble of sharpening those farm tools. The tools didn't even belong to Papa. They belonged to the man who owned the farm. Besides all that, they were moving to the mountains soon and Papa wouldn't even be using those tools anymore.

"That's not the point, Annie," Papa explained later. "Whoever farms this land in the spring is gonna need good, sharp tools to work with. It's just the respectable thing to do."

Winter's cold breath seemed to drag on endlessly until Annie began to think that it would last forever. Then, one morning as she and Ellie made their way to the barn to watch Papa feed the animals, she spotted some small specks of yellow along the path.

"Dandelions, Ellie! It's dandelions! That means that it's spring for sure, 'cause dandelions don't go bloomin' in the winter!"

Quicker than you could say "scat!" Annie reached down and snatched the tiny yellow flowers in one hand and raced to the barn to show Papa.

"Papa, Papa! It's spring. It's finally spring. These here dandelions are bloomin'. It's time to move to the mountains!"

"Well, bless my britches, Annie! I expect we'll be hearing from Granddaddy pert near any day now. He always plants his crops by the signs of the moon. Root crops like taters get planted first, on the dark of the moon. And the dark of the moon is just around the corner. You and Ellie better start watching for the mailman. Yep! I expect we'll hear from Granddaddy any day now," Papa repeated.

In the days that followed, Annie and Ellie sped through their morning chores and took up their posts at the front window, each one trying to be the first to spot the mailman as he rumbled up the graveled road making his appointed stops.

Rarely did Annie's family receive any mail, and so when the mailman's dusty Model A drew to a stop beside their mailbox just before noon one day, Annie and Ellie locked hands and danced around, nearly tripping over each other in their excitement.

"I saw him put a letter in the box!" cried Ellie.

"Well, what are we waitin' for?" asked Annie, already on her way out the front door and down the drive to the mailbox.

Hardly had the postman deposited the letter into the old, rusty mailbox before Annie snatched it back out and scurried back up the rocky driveway. She dared not open it, for it was addressed to Papa. Annie knew that it was not polite to open someone else's mail. But it only took a quick glance at the large scrawling letters on the front of the envelope to know it was Granddaddy's handwriting. But the waiting was not over. Papa and the boys were out on the farm and would not be home until later that evening.

Finally, just as the evening sun was dipping below the horizon, Papa and the boys came stomping in the back door. Papa barely had time to pull off his coat and hang his hat on the nail by the door before Annie ran rushing up with the letter in her outstretched hand.

"Open it, Papa! It's from Granddaddy. Let's see when he's comin', Papa!"

The children watched in eager anticipation as Papa pulled the letter from the envelope and began reading it silently.

"Read it out loud, Papa," begged Ellie. "When's he comin' to get us?"

"Well, I can tell you this much, Little Bit. You'd better help Mama start packin', 'cause this here is Tuesday, and Granddaddy's comin' for us on Saturday."

Unlike the winter days that dragged on like slow molasses, the next three days flew by. Mama had already been packing some of their belongings into cardboard boxes after the girls were in bed at night. And, as usual, it didn't take long to pack what few clothes and household items they owned.

When Annie and Ellie heard the sound of Granddaddy's truck chugging up the road early Saturday morning, they raced eagerly out to meet him. How good it was to see Grand-daddy's snow-white beard and twinkling blue eyes and hear his hearty laughter.

"Whoa now, girls! Don't break these stiff ole bones of mine with all that huggin' and squeezin'. We got some packin' up to do before we can head to the mountains!"

Dan and Paul were just as glad to see Granddaddy as were the girls. But they thought they were too big for all that hugging business, so they just stood there grinning like opossums while Granddaddy slapped them on the back and ruffled their hair in greeting.

Papa, Mama, and Granddaddy sat down inside just long enough to catch up on family news since their last visit, and to let Granddaddy rest for a little bit after his long trip down from the mountains.

Soon it was time to load the truck. Mama warned the girls to "make themselves scarce" so as not to be in the way of the men loading the truck.

Annie and Ellie took this opportunity to run down to the barn one last time to say goodbye to the animals. Mr. O'Cal-la owned the farm on Cornwallis Road and the animals as well. He had let Papa keep the milk from the cows in return for taking care of them and the other animals in the barn over the winter. Annie and Ellie patted Nellie on her cold, wet nose and rubbed Ginger's huge brown belly. Then the girls wished them both a fond farewell and hurried back up the path to the house.

Granddaddy did not drive. So he had hired the owner of the truck to bring him down to the flatlands to collect the family. It was a large white truck with a cab overhead where Mama and the girls could crawl up and rest or take a nap along the way. There was only room inside the cab for the driver and two others. So Granddaddy and Papa climbed into the front with the driver while the rest of the family made themselves as comfortable as they could amongst the boxes in the back. Mama had placed some quilts around to make the seating as comfortable as she could for the long journey.

Annie wondered how long it would be before she returned to the flatlands, or even if she ever would.

*Ellie'n me have had us some good times over these last few years. There've been some hard times shore enough, but there's one thing I do know! I'm off on a brand new kind of adventure with my best buddy, Ellie-Belly. And we're gonna be all right! Yessiree! We are gonna be all right!*

"Keep your eyes peeled for them cows, Ellie-Belly!" shouted Annie over the roar of the truck motor. And with that she burst into joyful song:

"She'll be comin' 'round the mountain when she comes! She'll be comin' 'round the mountain when she comes!"

# Acknowledgments

It is with love and a deep sense of gratitude that I acknowledge the faithful support of my late husband, Freddie Swindle, who passed away suddenly before seeing this book in print. Thank you, honey, for encouraging me every step of the way, and for always being just as excited as I was every time I heard from my editors. You were truly the wind beneath my wings.

Thanks to Brad Pauquette and his awesome team at Columbus Publishing Lab. Your expert advice and constructive feedback were always delivered in a prompt, courteous, and professional manner. Choosing you to publish my work was heaven-sent.

Finally, I thank God, my Heavenly Father, who assures me that I can do all things through Jesus Christ who gives me strength. (Philippians 4:13)